Emily Harvale lives in Eas
– although she would p̶r̶—— ̶—̶ ̶—̶—̶ ̶—̶ ̶—̶—̶
French Alps ... or Canada ... or anywhere that
has several months of snow. Emily loves
snow almost as much as she loves Christmas.
Having worked in the City (London) for
several years, Emily returned to her home
town of Hastings where she spends her days
writing ... and wondering if it will ever snow.
You can contact her via her website,
Facebook or Instagram.
There is also a Facebook group where fans
can chat with Emily about her books, her
writing day and life in general. Details can be
found on Emily's website.

Author contacts:
www.emilyharvale.com
www.twitter.com/emilyharvale
www.facebook.com/emilyharvalewriter
www.instagram.com/emilyharvale

***

Scan the code above to see all Emily's books on
Amazon

Also by this author

The Golf Widows' Club
Sailing Solo
Carole Singer's Christmas
Christmas Wishes
A Slippery Slope
The Perfect Christmas Plan
Be Mine
It Takes Two
Bells and Bows on Mistletoe Row

Lizzie Marshall series:
Highland Fling – book 1
Lizzie Marshall's Wedding – book 2

Goldebury Bay series:
Ninety Days of Summer – book 1
Ninety Steps to Summerhill – book 2
Ninety Days to Christmas – book 3

Hideaway Down series:
A Christmas Hideaway – book 1
Catch A Falling Star – book 2
Walking on Sunshine – book 3
Dancing in the Rain – book 4

Hall's Cross series
Deck the Halls – book 1
The Starlight Ball – book 2

Michaelmas Bay series
Christmas Secrets in Snowflake Cove – book 1
Blame it on the Moonlight – book 2

Lily Pond Lane series
The Cottage on Lily Pond Lane – four-part serial
Part One – New beginnings
Part Two – Summer secrets

ISBN 978-1-909917-83-5

Published by Crescent Gate Publishing

Print edition published worldwide 2022
E-edition published worldwide 2022

Cover design by JR and Emily Harvale

Emily Harvale

Broken Hearts
and
Fresh Starts
at
Cove Café

CRESCENT GATE PUBLISHING

Acknowledgements

My grateful thanks go to the following:

Christina Harkness for her patience and care in editing this book.
My webmaster, David Cleworth who does so much more than website stuff.
My cover design team, JR.
Luke Brabants. Luke is a talented artist and can be found at: www.lukebrabants.com
My wonderful friends for their friendship and love. You know I love you all.
All the fabulous members of my Readers' Club. You help and support me in so many ways and I am truly grateful for your ongoing friendship. I wouldn't be where I am today without you.
My Twitter and Facebook friends, and fans of my Facebook author page. It's great to chat with you. You help to keep me (relatively) sane!

Map of Clementine Cove

There's an interactive map, with more details,
on my website: www.emilyharvale.com

For Portia.

Chapter 1

Marian Blythe would be the first to admit she had never been good with numbers. There were no school awards or prizes for achieving high marks in mathematics, lining her shelves. And even though she ran her own business and her thirty-sixth birthday loomed large on the horizon like some ominous cloud, nothing much had changed. She enjoyed doing her accounts as much as she enjoyed a visit to the dentist. Basically ... not at all.

But even Marian could work out that with more money going out of her bank account than coming in, coffee wasn't the only thing brewing in her beloved Cove Café. Serious trouble bubbled just beneath the surface.

Unpaid bills were stacking up, higher than her pile of 'Breakfast Special Pancakes'. And there were six pancakes in that ... along with four rashers of bacon, lashings of maple syrup, and mouth-wateringly creamy scrambled egg on the side.

Marian had stopped counting the red demands. She'd tossed the eighth one – unopened – into the wooden box marked, 'Things to do today' that sat on her kitchen worktop in her home above the café.

She had placed the decoupage-covered box there, with its pictures of beautiful flowers and brightly coloured butterflies and birds, as an aide-memoire. It contained lists of items she needed to re-order to keep her café thriving; of proposed exciting changes to her menu; of delicious-sounding recipes she intended to try, and details of upcoming events in the village or nearby.

It had proved more than useful over the years and, once upon a time, it had made her smile every morning as she filled the kettle and flicked the switch to make her first cup of coffee of the day.

Lately though, all it seemed to contain were bills, reminders, demands ... and more bills. Now it had the air of a miniature coffin rather than a box of daily prompts and treats to look forward to.

Cove Café was no longer thriving, it was surviving, and the changes to her menu were more from desperation to entice customers through the door than from excitement.

If things continued the way they had been going for the last year or so, her precious café might have to close.

Would have to close.

Marian could not bear the thought of that. What would she do then? She had no other skills or talents that she could think of. Cove Café was her whole life. It was not just her business; it was also her home.

Where would she live if the café closed and she had to sell her cottage? She loved her cosy, ruby-painted cottage. It sat on a tapering cliff, at the end of a row of colourful cottages overlooking the bay and the little marina of Clementine Cove, where sailboats bobbed on the tranquil water and waves lapped at the shore.

Even in February, when the sun shone and the sea sparkled – and the central heating was set to a pleasant 20 degrees centigrade – Marian could pretend she lived on the Côte d'Azur – in one of the upmarket resorts with a breathtaking view of the Mediterranean, and fine sandy beaches surrounded by vineyards and ancient pine trees. Not in a tiny village on the south-east coast of England with a sand and shingle beach and a bay overlooking the English Channel.

Clementine Cove was equally beautiful in its own way though, and thanks to the

Christmas tree farm run by the Jurys, it also had its fair share of pine trees. Although none were ancient ... and none resembled those dotted across the coastline of the Med. Sadly, there weren't any vineyards surrounding the village and it distinctly lacked the ambience of the French Riviera. Especially on a day such as this. And now she only turned the heating up to 20 degrees when customers came in.

Marian had been to the Med once, many years ago, when she was around fourteen-years-old, on a holiday with her parents. They had stayed at a campsite, not one of the luxury hotels in prime position on a bustling, cosmopolitan promenade, where the cafés, restaurants and expensive shops had taken Marian's breath away just by her glancing in the windows.

The campsite had been situated in the middle of nowhere, although the nearest town was called Grimaud. The name of that should have given her parents pause for thought. But it hadn't. Although Marian had to concede that the town itself was very pretty. The campsite – not so much.

The travel agent had promised them a dream holiday.

'The campsite is in the heart of the Gulf of Saint-Tropez,' she had said, with a smile as wide as a bay. 'It has views of the

Mediterranean you'll just die for, and direct access to the warm, fine sands of a beach that never seems to end.'

Marian and her parents had taken a family holiday every year since she was a baby, but this was to be the first holiday abroad. Marian's mum had always dreamed of visiting the famous beaches of Saint-Tropez, so she was immediately hooked.

But as they soon discovered, translated from sales speak to plain English, the travel agent's words turned out to mean that the campsite sat high on a hill, several kilometres from the nearest beach, which was hidden from view by a line of sand dunes, most of which looked man-made.

If you ignored the warning signs that advised you not to go beyond them, 'at the risk of life', and stood at the edge of a crumbling cliff, you could indeed see the sea. However, you would have needed the skills and determination of a mountain goat to be able to gain direct access to the sandy beach below.

Unless you fell off the cliff, of course.

In spite of that – and the fact that the Gulf of Saint-Tropez was far larger than Marian or her parents had expected and the beaches of Saint-Tropez were a good 15 kilometres away, obscured by a promontory – Marian had a wonderful holiday, as did her parents. So much so that they all talked of going back, albeit to a different campsite.

Life, sadly, had other ideas. That was to be the last holiday Marian and her parents took together.

Even after all these years, Marian still missed those family holidays.

Almost as much as she missed her parents.

They had been late to parenthood, but early to their graves.

Her dad had died of a sudden heart attack one week before Marian's seventeenth birthday, and not long after, her mum had followed, ending almost three years of battling cancer. A tumour had been discovered four months after their return from that final holiday, and everything had changed.

'I've lived a full life,' Marian's mum had whispered, as her breathing grew more difficult. 'No need to weep for me, my darling. Smile when you think of your dad and me. He loved us both with all his heart and I'm longing to see him again. I'm so sorry to be leaving you, but we'll be watching over you. I hope one day you'll find a man you will love as much as I have loved your dad, and who will love you as much as your dad has loved me. And when you find him, darling, don't ever let him go.'

Marian's teenaged-mind had instantly conjured up an image of Archer Rhodes, although she had rapidly dismissed it. They were friends; nothing more.

'I love you, Mum,' Marian had said, fighting back a tsunami of tears so as not to add to her mum's distress. 'There's no need to worry about me. I'll keep you and Dad right here in my heart so we'll never be far apart. And whatever happens, I can promise you one thing ... I will be fine.'

If only that were true.

Her parents had left her the cottage and a small amount of money, and Stella Pinkheart, her mum's best friend, had been her temporary guardian, but Marian needed to earn a living.

The idea of running a café from her home had not been hers; it had been suggested to her by Stella. Not that Stella, a retired school teacher, knew much about how Marian should do that, and Marian had poo-pooed such a fanciful notion.

The seed, however, grew. Besides, Marian had no clue as to what else she could do. She might not be good with numbers but she had baked since she was a small child and everyone loved the cakes she made. How hard could running a café be? All she would need to do was bake cakes and make teas and coffees.

Looking back, she often wondered how she could have been so naïve.

Nevertheless, with a lot of help from Stella, Marian's friends and the rest of the locals, plus a good deal of luck, Marian made a business plan and eventually obtained planning consent for a change of use of the cottage. She opened Cove Café on her nineteenth birthday.

She had never expected her business to make her a pot of gold but she had hoped it would give her a comfortable living. Or at the very least, allow her to keep her head above water, which it had done for many years.

Right now though, things were looking grim. At this rate she would be lucky to keep the 'Welcome to Cove Café, we're open', sign on the pink front door, until Easter; let alone until the real rush started in the summer. Soon the only sound coming from the bell above the door would be a death knell, not the cheery tinkling tune it currently played.

The snow storms in December had kept many customers away. Although none of them seemed to have too much trouble making the trip to Millside, the shopping centre that sat on the outskirts of Clementine Cove on the former site of an old mill.

A few of her regulars had made the effort and supported her. Stella popped in as often as she could to say hello and have a cup of builder's strength tea in one of Marian's poshest, porcelain cups and saucers. Sometimes she stayed for half an hour; sometimes for a lot longer. She always had gossip to share, or some snippet of information, often concerning Rosie Parker, the Reverend William Parker's sister. Stella and Rosie, were supposed to be good friends, but from the way they talked about each other, you would not know it. It was Stella who first thought up the nickname, Nosy, as in Nosy Parker, for Rosie. Stella declared it was a slip of the tongue but she had smiled somewhat wickedly as she had said it.

Newcomers, Elodie Abbott and Iris Talbot were frequent visitors to the café, as was Marian's life-long friend, Archer. Marian still found it hard to believe that Iris was Stanley Talbot's niece. Few people in the village had liked Stanley. And with good reason. Although, in the end, it transpired that even Stanley had a good side to him. Now that he was dead.

It was even more strange to comprehend all that had happened since Elodie and Iris had arrived. So much had changed since Christmas.

Marian let out a sigh and stared out of one of the windows of the café. The sky was so dark that it seemed as if it were evening, not mid-morning. Across the bay, the lights were on in the church of St Mary's in the Wood – a small Norman church perched near the edge of the steep and rocky cliff known as Hope Head. Rosehip Cottage, the rectory, nestled behind the church and was only just visible, along with the lanes of several pretty, pastel-coloured cottages.

To the right of Hope Head stood the lighthouse, at the mouth of Clementine Cove, just behind Arrow Point, an equally rocky but less steep promontory directly opposite Hope Head. The lighthouse was now owned by the King family and rented out as a Bed and Breakfast, but the light was still operational although remotely controlled these days. It was certainly a beacon of hope today, its light flashing brightly through the torrential rain.

Marian gave it a cursory glance, focusing her attention on the bright blue façade and thatched roof of Archer Rhodes' pub, The Bow and Quiver. It sat on Arrow Point beside a small copse and more lanes of cottages and larger houses.

Archer was no doubt getting on with his day. Not a single thought of Marian and what she might be doing so much as entering his head for a second. Marian was pretty sure of that. Now all his time seemed to be taken up with Elodie. But Marian couldn't blame him.

That's what people did when they were in love.

Yet another thing to dampen Marian's spirits. Archer had been her own beacon of hope. That light went out at Christmas when he fell head over heels in love with Elodie.

Marian had tried to be pleased for Archer. They had been friends their entire lives; they still were. Archer had told her just last week that nothing would ever change that. But things had changed. Before Elodie came on the scene, Archer popped into Cove Café every day and bought a coffee and a muffin or a bacon sandwich or just some toast. Sometimes he bought them to take away; sometimes he had them in the café, but every time he stopped and chatted for a while. Now his visits were becoming less frequent and when he did pop in, Elodie was usually by his side.

Marian liked Elodie. The problem was, although she had never admitted it to anyone, not even to herself, Marian loved Archer. A rather disturbing but true fact she had only acknowledged at Christmas.

She had always known he held a special place in her heart, but she had not realised, until he and Elodie became an item, quite how special a place. When Archer told her he had fallen in love with Elodie, it had hit her like a train at full speed and it knocked the life out of her for several days.

How could she have been in love with Archer Rhodes and not have known it?

But she had known it. Deep down. She had simply never wanted to admit it. It was a secret she had buried so deeply that no one knew how she felt.

Except that wasn't entirely true. One person had known how she felt.

Stanley Talbot.

That was something else that happened at Christmas.

Stanley had lived in the village for several years. Marian could not recall how many, exactly. Or when he had moved to Clementine Cove. He had seemed pleasant enough at first, from what Marian could remember. He chatted to the locals, made friends with the Reverend and Rosie. He even joined the choir. But there was something about him that made the villagers begin to feel uneasy.

Of course, they had given him the benefit of the doubt ... until some of the villagers said they felt there was something unnerving about the way Stanley seemed to watch them. Plus, he asked a great deal of questions. And he carried a notebook with him everywhere he went and was often scribbling away as people chatted or went about their day. Some said they were certain he'd taken photos of them when he thought they weren't looking. Many were certain he was up to no good. Several were convinced something bad would come of it. But no one knew exactly what.

At least not until Christmas Eve, when Stanley sent Marian a message from the grave. Well, a message via a parcel courier, along with a beautifully wrapped gift. A gift that contained a file with Marian's name on it. And as Marian soon discovered, that file contained details that she thought no one knew about her. Secrets she was certain she had kept hidden. Yet somehow, Stanley had known them all. It was as if he had read her mind. And it was terrifying.

It was, however, a huge relief because Stanley Talbot was dead. At the time she did not know that quite a few people had also received a beautifully wrapped file. Although when Marian had received hers, she had known at once that she probably was not the only one to be given such a surprising gift. It was a day or two later that she discovered how and why.

On Christmas Eve, a number of files had been delivered; each one to the person named on its tab, together with Stanley's best wishes and apologies for the way he had behaved. Like Marian's, each had a card attached that had read, "With the compliments of the season and good wishes for a Happy New Year from Stanley Talbot."

Elodie and Iris, who had attended Stanley's funeral, had told her all about it. They had met a woman after the funeral service and she had explained it all. She and Stanley had been in love and Stanley had changed his ways because of it. The files were sent as per his final request.

It sounded very odd, and frankly, rather bewildering to Marian, but all she really cared about was that apparently no one else had read her file. Or so the accompanying note had stated, and Elodie and Iris had confirmed they believed that to be the case. They, themselves had seen the files, but neither one had read them.

Over the ensuing weeks, one or two other residents of the village had admitted to receiving such a present on Christmas Eve. Some laughed nervously; some said their files were just one page of nonsense. Others, like Archer, said their file had been a blessing. Some of the files had disclosed information to the recipient of which they, themselves had been completely unaware.

As in the case of Archer.

He was more than happy to tell all and sundry what his file had contained. Details and the whereabouts of his long-lost child. A child he had searched for his entire adult life. A child he had been told had died, but definitely hadn't. A child who was now a teenager, and who he would soon be travelling to Australia to meet. With Elodie by his side.

Marian had been happy for Archer on that score. She had known about his child for as long as he had himself. Or almost as long. Although he had not completely confided in her about it. He had not really confided in anyone, other than his parents. Archer liked to keep things close to his chest.

Not that Marian could talk. She had been keeping secrets for just as long. And yet Stanley Talbot had known each and every one of them.

And not just her secrets, of course, as several of the residents of Clementine Cove discovered. No one knew how Stanley had acquired the knowledge he had, or how he had known so many people's deepest, darkest secrets. But he had definitely known them. At least he had definitely known all of Marian's.

Marian shook her head and dragged her gaze back to her laptop, where a row of red figures ran down one column of her accounts sheet, like blood trickling from her veins.

She slammed the lid of the laptop shut and heaved out a heavy sigh. Her life had become so depressing.

This weather didn't help. Rain pelted the roof, filling the gutters so fast they overflowed, like a garden water feature – only not as attractive. A curtain of rain ran down the windows and over the sills, forming rivers between the cracks in the pavement that wound their way to the gutters in the road. The water had nowhere to go from there; the drains were full to bursting and had been since all the snow had melted in January. And it had rained virtually non-stop all that month.

February seemed to be intent on doing the same. It was more than half way through the month and Marian could not recall seeing more than one single day of sunshine. Just one day, a couple of days ago. Oddly enough, it had been on Valentine's Day.

Not that it had been a particularly 'sunny' day for Marian. Especially when she popped in to The Bow and Quiver pub and saw the huge bunch of red roses that Archer had bought for Elodie. He'd had them delivered to the pub because that was where Elodie spent most of her time these days.

She had as good as moved in. Much to Marian's consternation. Elodie rarely returned to her home and the family business in London now. She was supposed to have been staying in Clementine Cottage – Stanley Talbot's former home – along with Iris, Stanley's niece, who had also decided to transfer her residence and her business to Clementine Cove since Christmas. But from what Marian could see, Elodie was rarely anywhere other than the pub.

Marian should not moan about the newcomers though. Without the visits of Elodie and Iris, she would have even fewer customers.

Bad weather and freezing temperatures kept most of the villagers indoors, it seemed. Curled up in front of their fires after making their own tea, coffee or hot chocolates. Why would they want to walk or drive to Cove Café? Even if they parked in Cove Close, they would get soaked to the skin getting from their cars to the café, often battered by gale force winds. It was far more convenient for them to go to one of the cafés at Millside if they did venture out. They could drive to the covered car park on site, or catch a bus and get off right outside the sliding front doors to the shopping centre. Marian could hardly blame them for preferring to do that.

But if Marian's takings did not pick up, there would not be a café at the cove to come to. How would the villagers feel about that? Would they even care? Would they try to help her if they knew how bad things were? Should she finally open up about some of her money problems? Maybe Archer could give her some advice? He ran his own business. He would understand.

No. He would probably offer to help her out financially, and she could not allow him to do that. Especially now he had found his long-lost daughter and was planning an expensive trip to visit her.

Especially now he was with Elodie.

Maybe Marian should confide in Stella?

No. She could not do that either. Stella would simply tell her to try harder and things would all work out. That mindset had not helped Marian with her maths in school; it would not help her now.

'Everything happens for a reason,' Marian's mum had always said, along with, 'Ask the Universe, and it will provide.'

If everything happened for a reason, Marian could not wait to discover what the reason was for her present state of affairs. As long as it was something good. But based on the way her life had been going lately, it did not bode well.

Perhaps, right now, asking the Universe might be Marian's only hope.

But today, just like every other day, she would fix a cheery-looking smile in place and offer a warm welcome and a jokey comment to anyone brave enough to combat this awful weather and open the pink front door of Cove Café.

She turned the Closed sign to Open and looked out again across the bay.

What was the harm in asking?

She closed her eyes tight and then opened them, smiling hopefully at the gunmetal sky.

'Universe. Please send me a way to get out of the mess I'm in. And, if it's not too much trouble, sooner rather than later, would be good.'

Chapter 2

He should have waited a few more days.

Only an inexperienced sailor would leave the safety of the marina and venture down the East coast of England towards the English Channel when there were severe weather warnings. And Parker Sanderson was not inexperienced. He had been sailing since he could walk; and he had been walking at nine months old – thirty-eight years ago. Give or take a month or two.

The problem was, he had needed to get away from Broadlands Bay as soon as possible. And definitely before the bells of St Benedict's rang out. He had thought he could tough-it-out. He had been through worse things and survived.

Hadn't he?

As the sun came up each day, followed all too quickly by the moon and the night, it slowly dawned on him that he had never been through anything quite as bad as this.

Everywhere he looked, he saw her. Saw what his life might have been like if she had stayed with him ... and not run off with his best mate instead.

Not that she had actually run off. That was half the problem. He almost wished she had. At least then he wouldn't have to see her every bloody day. Or have to fight back the urge to punch his former best mate on the nose. Or pretend to be fine with what was happening.

How could anyone expect him to be fine with it?

'You're better off without her, son,' his dad had pronounced.

'It's a good thing you found out the truth about the type of woman she is.' His mum had pursed her lips and shaken her head. 'She had us all fooled, darling. Not just you. We all believed she was perfect.'

'No such thing as perfect.' His gran had wagged a bony finger in his direction. 'You come close, my boy,' she had added, with a crooked grin. A grin that he had apparently inherited.

And had not used much since he had discovered the truth about his girlfriend, Isabella.

'We didn't plan to fall in love,' Greg, his former best mate, had confessed. 'It just sort of happened.'

For a split second, Parker had wanted to kill them both. Not that he would ever have done so.

'You were always working on that damn boat,' Isabella had said, pointing an accusatory finger at Parker's beloved yacht. 'You didn't even notice I was there half the time. What did you expect?'

'My best friend to have my back. And my girlfriend to be faithful.' Parker had felt numb.

Was that too much to ask? It seemed it was.

Nevertheless, he still could not quite believe that this was happening. He had foolishly hoped that Isabella would come running back. Or that Greg would realise his friendship with Parker was more important. Neither of those things had happened.

Instead, Isabella Montford and Gregory Bowen-Smythe were tying the knot at 2 p.m. precisely. On sodding Valentine's Day. A fact that had made Parker even more certain he wanted to punch his best mate. And he might just have done so if he had remained on dry land.

'It won't last,' his gran had said. 'One should never get married on a Monday.'

'Isn't it bad luck to move house on a Monday?' his mum had added.

The only reason the wedding was on a Monday was because, in their haste to wed, Isabella and Greg had booked the very first date they could.

Parker had known Greg all his life, and dated Isabella for five years. Yet he did not really know either of them very well. Or so he had discovered. Because not for one second would he ever have imagined either of them could behave in such a way. Now he had lost them both, and the thought of having to spend as much as one more day in the little seaside town of Broadlands Bay had filled him with dread. And an increasing urge to flatten Greg.

But why risk humiliation, arrest and a possible sentence, or at the very least, a fine and community service, when he could, instead, get on board his very own motor yacht and sail away into the sunset?

Well, sunrise. But that didn't have the same ring to it. Not that anyone could see the sun through the mass of black, ominous-looking clouds that had rolled up the coast that day and hung heavy around the Northumberland shores and particularly over Broadlands Bay all morning.

At least he had the satisfaction of knowing it would probably rain on Isabella and Greg's Big Day. And then he felt guilty for being so mean-spirited.

His crew of three had been none too happy to be leaving in such a rush.

'The weather's looking dodgy?' Jasper, his bosun had pointed out.

'Thanks for the precise report.' Parker hated it when people stated the obvious.

'I'm just saying, man. Maybe we should wait it out and see what tomorrow brings.' Jasper threw him a sheepish smile and added a slight shrug for good measure. 'Why the sudden rush?'

Tomorrow would bring pictures of the happy couple, and tales of the wedding, the reception and more. Parker did not intend to stick around for that. He would rather face a raging storm than all the sympathetic smiles that he knew would be coming his way.

'Poor Parker,' everyone would say. 'His heart must be breaking.'

They would be right.

Isabella had been the love of his life. Or so he had thought. She was the woman he had assumed he would have a family with. Grow old with. After all, they had been together for five years.

How stupid could he be?

'We've been drifting apart for at least a year,' Isabella had told him, just three short months ago.

That had been news to him. He had believed they were sailing along rather nicely. He had even decided that, perhaps, it was time that he proposed. Isabella had been dropping hints for at least the last three years, although he had to admit, she had not done so for a long time. They had been living together for some while. And now that he was finally close to achieving his dream, this was as good a time as any. The motor yacht he had been repairing and working on for the last two years was finished and ready to sail.

It had always been his dream to have his own luxury motor yacht but he had never dared to believe it might be possible. They were not exactly cheap. But he had worked hard and saved even harder; taken any odd job he could get to boost his earnings as a sales executive at his father's small, luxury car showroom. He had mown lawns, washed cars, walked dogs when he was younger. As he'd grown, he had built garden sheds and summerhouses, repaired cars, still walked dogs, and added a host of other services and skills to increase his growing bank balance. But it would still have taken him many more years to be able to afford a yacht.

Luckily for him, he had been bequeathed a substantial sum of money in a will. It had come as a complete surprise. A huge surprise, in fact. He had known Jack Thorpe was a sailor. He had known Jack had once owned his own yacht. But Parker had never seen a photo and Jack had never given Parker as much as a hint of what size or type of yacht it was. In fact, Jack had hardly said much to Parker at all.

Since the age of five, Parker had done odd jobs for Jack, who lived in a gated mansion on a plot of land almost the same size as Broadlands Bay itself. Jack hadn't really needed Parker's assistance; he was fit and healthy and more than capable of doing those jobs himself. Or more likely to pay a skilled professional or tradesman to do them for him. But like most people in Broadlands Bay, Jack knew Parker was keen to earn extra pocket money and he always seemed to find another job for Parker to do.

Until Jack was seriously injured in a motorbike accident and had to spend the last years of his life in a wheelchair. He genuinely needed Parker's help after that.

Parker often told Jack about his dream of owning his own yacht one day. Jack told Parker to chase that dream. Then Jack had unexpectedly passed away and shortly afterwards, a firm of solicitors had told Parker of his good fortune.

Jack had left Parker a substantial bequest. More than one million pounds. Enough for Parker to buy himself a yacht. A small, brand new motor yacht. Or a larger but still classy second-hand boat. Or a much larger, luxury motor yacht but one that required some work. Much to Isabella's dismay, Parker had chosen the latter. He had been working on it ever since.

Now Parker's dream had become a reality. He had shared that dream with Isabella and believed she was totally on board. It was all planned out.

Isabella, it seemed, had decided she had other plans.

'Are you saying we should take a break?' he had asked, fighting down the hurt and surprise and fear when she had first made him aware there was a problem.

'No, Parker,' she had replied, all dewy-eyed and beautiful, and Parker had sighed with relief. But before the last gasp of breath had escaped him, Isabella added, 'Not a break. An end. It's best for both of us. It's over, Parker. We both need to move on.'

'Move on?' He couldn't quite take in what she was telling him. 'I ... I don't understand. Are you saying you don't love me anymore?'

The softest of sighs left her cupid's bow lips. 'I'm not certain I ever really loved you, Parker. I'm not trying to be cruel. Just honest. You're a great guy and one day you'll find someone who loves you as you deserve. Sadly, that's not me.'

But she hadn't been honest, had she? She'd omitted to tell him that she'd been sleeping with his best friend for two weeks prior to this sudden realisation that she didn't love him. It wasn't until a week after she'd dumped him that he'd discovered that little nugget of gold. Greg hadn't been able to hide the truth. Guilt got the better of him and he blurted the whole thing out.

'Now I've asked her to marry me. And she's said yes. I'm so sorry, mate. Believe me. The last thing either of us wanted was to hurt you. But things have a way of happening, don't they? And maybe it's for the best. Isabella doesn't really like the sea.'

That, along with everything else, was news to Parker. Isabella had told him she loved the idea of sailing around the Med. But then again, Isabella had also told him that she loved him.

Next time, he would be more careful.

Next time?

There wouldn't be a next time. Now he would devote his entire time to his yacht.

But he was still in love with Isabella.

Sadly, Isabella was not in love with him.

Which was why he had needed to leave Broadlands Bay. And he had needed to leave before the wedding. Failing that, he might very well dash headlong into that sodding church and shout at the top of his voice, 'Stop! Don't marry Greg. Run away with me.'

That would only have made him look and feel more foolish.

No. Stormy seas were a more appealing prospect.

And so, in spite of the weather forecast, he and his yacht, *The Dream*, along with his crew of three headed out into the North Sea and down towards the English Channel.

Now though, the sea did appear to be getting far stormier than predicted. Maybe Jasper had been right. They had left Broadlands Bay just two days ago and already Parker needed to return to dry land. Or at least find a safe harbour for his yacht before the weather turned far worse. Right now, *The Dream* – both Parker's and the boat itself – were at risk of running aground.

Chapter 3

'Morning, Iris.'

Marian's friendly welcome was genuine. She could do with cheering up and Iris had one of those smiles that made you want to return it, no matter what kind of mood you were in.

'Morning, Marian!'

Iris shoved the door closed behind her and leant against it, removing her lime green bobble hat and shaking out her glossy red fringe. The long, dangly earrings that seemed to be giraffes, danced about her shoulders and she smiled at Marian as she shrugged off her purple coat.

'Bit blowy out there?' Marian grinned, as she asked the obvious.

She scooped up her laptop and the batch of papers from the table where she had been working. Iris liked to sit by the window, and although there were two windows fronting the café, and therefore two window-tables, this was the one Iris and her best friend Elodie always seemed to choose.

'You're not kidding! I don't think I'll ever get used to how windy it gets down here. It's blowing a gale. I almost ended up on my bum when I got out of Bentley's truck. I could hardly stand. Oh. Please don't move for me, Marian. I can sit somewhere else. Or join you, if that's okay.'

Marian hesitated for just a second.

'It's fine.' She tucked her laptop and papers firmly under one arm. 'I need to get on with other things anyway. How's Bentley?'

Bentley was the gorgeous, blond-haired hunk who worked as a chef at The Bow and Quiver. He and Iris had been dating on and off since Christmas. Clearly, they were 'on' again at the moment.

Iris shrugged and grinned. 'He's good.'

'I wasn't asking about his performance in the sack,' Marian joked, grinning back. 'I was asking about his health.'

Iris laughed. 'He's good on that front too. How're you?' She glanced around the café. 'Rushed off your feet again, I see.'

Marian's smile slipped a fraction but she forced it back into position.

'You've just missed the ravenous hordes. And The Great Unwashed never get up until after 11, according to Nosy Parker, so you're a few minutes early to get trampled on by them.'

The Great Unwashed were the newcomers to the village who lived in the box-like, identical houses that made up the new housing estate near Moneymaker Circle. Not that the estate was that new. It had been there for at least ten years now.

Rosie Parker, the Reverend's sister, was against the estate being built, as were some of the other residents of Clementine Cove, but in spite of their increasingly vociferous opposition, their objections were overruled and the houses shot up within a matter of months.

Everyone seemed to move in at once as soon as the houses hit the market; some had sold off-plan and the others were snapped up within days. Rosie, rather meanly, labelled the in-comers, 'The Great Unwashed' and although Marian knew it was wrong, she did think it was quite amusing. But then she had always had an odd sense of humour.

Iris gave her a scolding look, accompanied by one of her smiles.

'You really shouldn't call them that, Marian.'

'I know. I just can't help myself. I must try harder. Anyway, what can I get you?'

'One of your delicious, raspberry and white chocolate muffins, please. And a cappuccino. I'm meeting El, so we'll ... oh. Speak of the devil.'

The door flew open and Elodie, looking somewhat bedraggled, swept inside. Just as Iris had, she leant against the door once she had closed it.

'Bloody hell! If I'd known how bad it was out there, I'd have taken Archer up on his offer of a lift, instead of laughing at him for suggesting it. The pub's probably less than half a mile from this door, but on a day like today, that's half a mile too far. I'm drenched.'

'Is it raining?' Marian quipped as the torrential rain battered the windows and poured down the panes, overflowing from the gutters.

Elodie grinned. 'Just a bit.' She wasn't wearing a hat and her, usually perfectly tonged, auburn waves with gold and chestnut lowlights, looked as if she had just stepped out of the shower. 'I don't suppose I could borrow a towel, could I?'

'Of course.'

Marian dashed to the kitchen, returning with a clean hand towel, which she handed to Elodie as they met at the table in the window. Elodie peeled off her raincoat and hung it on a hook nearby, nodding her thanks to Marian as she wiped her face and hair.

'Why couldn't we meet at the pub?' Elodie asked Iris, scowling, but in a good-natured manner.

'Because you need to get out more. It's as if you and Archer are glued together.' Iris was grinning.

Elodie pulled out the chair opposite her best friend and sat down.

'We're in love.'

'Sickeningly so.'

'You can talk. You couldn't keep your hands off Bentley in the pub last night.'

'We're in lust ... again.'

Elodie laughed. 'Yeah, well, you'd better let the man get some sleep. Archer said Bentley was nodding off over a pot of Watercress soup he was preparing yesterday. The poor guy is exhausted.'

'What can I say? Valentine's Day. Or should I say, night? Was a particularly good one.'

Elodie shook her head and glanced up at Marian.

'Help me talk some sense into her, will you? One minute she says it's over between her and Bentley, the next, she's attached to him like a limpet. The poor guy doesn't know if he's coming or going.'

'Now that could be a problem,' Marian said. She was about to add a crude comment but Iris spoke up before she had a chance to continue.

'I can't decide. He's definitely not 'The One'. I can tell you that for certain. But he's pretty good as 'the one right now'. Besides, I didn't want to spend Valentine's Day without a man, so we got back together for a couple of days. You can't shoot me for that. No one wants to be alone at Valentine's.'

'Some of us didn't have a choice,' Marian said, rather more acerbically than she'd intended. 'So, what can I get you, Elodie? Iris is having a muffin.' She grinned. 'I could make a joke about that. But I won't. D'you want something hot?'

'She's left Archer in the pub,' Iris quipped.

Marian couldn't argue with that. Archer was definitely hot, with a smile warm enough to melt the biggest iceberg. He was tall, strapping and broad shouldered with the looks of a movie star and dark hair of the richest brown, to match.

Marian shook away the image of him forming in her mind's eye and gave a little cough.

'Sadly, he's not on the menu.'

'I fancy a sausage sandwich.' Elodie pulled a face and hurried on. 'No comments from either of you, please.'

'Spoilsport.' Iris winked at Marian. 'As if either of us would comment on that.'

'Right. Give me a moment to take this stuff back upstairs,' Marian said, raising her arm slightly to show her laptop and papers tucked beneath. Not that they were hidden, exactly. 'I was trying to catch up on my accounts, but it's a thankless task.'

'We'll hold the fort,' Iris said, as Marian turned away.

'Thanks. But other than you two, I think it'll be a quiet day. I'm not expecting a rush.'

'Is that one of those superyachts?'

Elodie sounded surprised, and Marian glanced back over her shoulder, peering through the windows out towards the bay to where Elodie was pointing.

'It looks like one,' Iris confirmed. 'Although from here it looks like a toy boat in a bath tub of swirling bubbles.'

The boat was entering the mouth of the cove and appeared to be bouncing off the crests of some exceedingly high waves. Marian, Iris and Elodie all watched silently until the boat sailed into smoother waters.

Marian let out the breath she knew she had been holding, thankful the boat was now safe, and equally thankful she wasn't on it.

'Definitely a superyacht,' Iris said, now that it had come closer. 'And a luxury one by the look of it. Although I suppose, by definition, all superyachts are luxury yachts. Look at those sleek lines.'

'That's what everyone says about me,' Marian joked. She raised her brows and pinched at least an inch of excess weight around her waist with her free hand.

'You're gorgeous, Marian,' Elodie said. 'I have no idea how you're still single.'

'It's a mystery.' Marian averted her eyes. 'Be back in a mo.' She raced upstairs via the door that accessed her living space and tossed the laptop on the sofa in her sitting room. 'It's because you've stolen the man I love!'

She hadn't meant to shriek and the strength of her emotions took her by surprise. Thankfully, neither Elodie nor Iris would have heard her. She glared at her reflection in the mirror. She was a little overweight but she wasn't fat by any means. People often said she was pretty. She liked her hair. It reminded her of hot chocolate. Her skin looked a bit pale. But it was February, after all. She longed for the summer and the months of sunshine. And the mass of tourists. But that was a different issue. She looked prettier with a tan. Archer had told her once, that he thought she was beautiful. It was when he was consoling her after another of her disastrous romances had come to an end. She had not had that many romances, but none of them had worked out.

'Any man would be lucky to have you,' he had said.

Any man but him, it seemed. He had never even tried to kiss her. Not once.

'Get a grip, Marian Blythe. You're not a teenager. You're a grown woman. And Elodie didn't steal Archer. He walked away of his own accord.'

Chapter 4

That was a close shave.

Parker did not try to hide the relief he felt when the anchor hit the seabed in the safety of the bay. He had never heard of Clementine Cove but when he had seen it on the chart, and had spotted the beam from the lighthouse, he was mighty glad it was there. He had never known a storm to peak so fast. Another half an hour of that and *The Dream* – and *his* dream might very well have been on the bottom of the English Channel.

He had been a damn fool to start this voyage when he had. He knew it and so did his crew. There had been rumblings before they had set out. Jasper had even asked him if he wouldn't rather wait until the weather had cleared, but nope. Parker Sodding Sanderson knew best.

Parker cursed himself under his breath.

'Risk your own life if you want, you stupid bastard, but don't risk the lives of your crew.'

He clawed his fingers through his thick, blond hair and let out a long breath.

They were not just crew; they were close friends. And he had already lost two people he had considered friends. He would rather not lose more.

'Safe and sound!' Jasper popped his head around the door of the bridge. He sounded as relieved as Parker felt, and maybe a little surprised. 'Not sure I could've got her in safely. Those waves were something else, man.'

'I owe you an apology.'

'Me?'

Parker nodded. 'We should've waited for a couple of days.'

Jasper shrugged. 'Hey. It is what it is. No harm done. We've found a safe harbour.' Jasper looked out at the cliffs and the sweep of the bay they had sailed into. 'Been here before?'

'Nope. Didn't know the place existed. Thankful that it does though. What would we sailors do without these?'

He tapped the display on the screen in front of him as a loud tut sounded from the behind.

'Drown, probably. You bloody moron.'

'What's up with you, Bel?' Jasper asked.

'What's up with me?' Bel glowered at Parker and glared at Jasper as she stomped up the stairs to the bridge. 'I'll tell you what's up with me. "Come with us, Bel," Parker said to me. "It'll be smooth sailing around the Med all summer." You failed to mention that you'd try to kill us all before we'd left the English Channel!'

'Ah,' said Parker. 'About that. Sorry.'

'Sorry?' Bel shrieked. 'Is that it? "Sorry." You will be, you moron. Believe me.'

'Er. You shouldn't speak to the captain like that.' Parker threw her one of his crooked grins.

'The captain is bloody lucky I'm speaking to him at all. What I wanted to do ... what I seriously considered doing ... was murdering you. Bloody captain, my arse. You're lucky you haven't got a mutiny on your hands.'

'Isn't this a mutiny?' Parker glanced at Jasper, unable to hide his amusement. He was so glad to be alive that nothing else seemed important.

'Search me,' Jasper said with another of his shrugs.

'What's all the racket about?' Nikki, the chief steward ... well, the only steward. And also, assistant deck crew and assistant engineer and first officer, yawned and scratched her head as she joined the rest of the crew. 'I was trying to get some sleep.'

Parker's mouth dropped open, along with Bel's and Jasper's. They all stared at Nikki in disbelief.

'Are you seriously telling us you slept through that?' Parker blinked and shook his head. He had sailed with Nikki many times and he knew she could fall asleep on a pinhead, but this was something else.

'Slept through what?' Nikki yawned again.

Jasper laughed and swept her off her feet in a bear hug.

'You're the best!' he exclaimed.

'Yeah, yeah. And you're a yeti.' Nikki pushed her way free but Jasper ruffled her hair with his hand, and then he did the same to Bel.

'Get off me, you prat!' Her eyes were like daggers. 'One of these days...' She did not finish her threat.

'Don't poke the bear when it's already in a strop,' Nikki said to Jasper.

'F-off,' Bel said.

'Now, now.' Parker smiled. 'Let's try to be professionals. We can't behave like this when we've got wealthy clients on board.'

'Are you going to try to drown them too?' Bel's tone dripped sarcasm.

'Where are we?' Nikki asked, glancing around. 'If this is the Med, I'm getting on the next boat to the Caribbean.'

'Welcome to Clementine Cove.' Parker stretched an arm out in front of him.

'You what?'

'Clementine Cove.'

'About as far from the Med as we can possibly be,' Bel added.

'Not true. We were farther away in Broadlands Bay,' Parker pointed out.

'And safer.' Bel narrowed her eyes at him.

'Why don't we get on dry land and stretch our legs? I'll buy breakfast,' Parker offered. Due to the weather conditions, he had been too busy steering the yacht to think about food and he hadn't eaten since last night.

'Aye, aye, Captain.' Jasper grinned broadly.

'That's the best idea I've heard since boarding this bloody boat,' said Bel.

'Is it morning?' Nikki queried. 'It looks pretty dark out there.'

'Because we're in the midst of a raging storm,' Bel bleated. 'It's almost midday.'

Nikki yawned again. She was still in her PJs.

'Give me five minutes to get dressed.'

Chapter 5

'They're heading this way!' Marian couldn't contain her surprise. Or her excitement.

How sad was that? How had things got so bad that the mere prospect of four potential customers coming to her café filled her with wonder and unadulterated happiness?

Well ... maybe not entirely unadulterated. If they did step over the threshold of Cove Café she would have to give Iris a sticky bun for free. But it was worth a sticky bun if the newbies ordered breakfasts.

Heck. At this stage, it didn't matter what they ordered. Whatever it was, it meant four customers Marian hadn't expected to have today. Whether it was pathetic or not, that was cause for excitement.

When Elodie had said it looked as if the people from the luxury yacht were getting off and heading for dry land, the last place

Marian expected such obviously wealthy types to patronise was her café. She assumed they would be picked up in a pre-ordered minicab, or possibly a chauffeur-driven limousine, and wafted away to the one really classy restaurant in Clementine Cove. The one overlooking the lake at Millside. Although even that might not be posh enough for owners of a luxury yacht. Nevertheless, you had to book in advance if you wanted a table at *Lac Bleu*. Not that Marian had ever been there. She definitely couldn't afford their prices. Nor could many of the villagers.

'They'll be going to *Lac Bleu*,' she had said.

'They'll be unlucky.' Elodie shook her head. 'It's closed for refurbishment. Valentine's night was their last service. That's why I was so thrilled Archer had managed to book us a table. And it was divine. But I've already told you that.'

'Several times,' Iris said, pulling a face. 'Maybe they're going to the pub. I'd definitely need a stiff drink – or five – if I'd been on that boat in those seas.'

'I know.' Elodie nodded. 'My heart was in my mouth just watching it manoeuvre into the bay. At one point I honestly thought it'd be swept onto the lighthouse rocks.'

'Me too.' Iris looked inappropriately gleeful at the thought of such an occurrence. 'And smashed into tiny pieces. The lifeboat would've had to be mustered to rescue the crew from the rocks. Although the captain would've gone down with his ship, obviously.'

'What?' Both Marian and Elodie stared at Iris. She at least had the decency to look a little shame-faced.

'Sorry. My imagination was running away with me. I watched *Titanic* again the other night. Blame that.'

'Oooooh! I love that film.' Elodie had a dreamy expression on her face.

'Really?' Marian shook her head. 'The hero died.'

'He died so that the heroine could live.' Elodie sounded defensive. 'That's so romantic.'

'They could've both lived. Nope. Not one of my favourites.'

'I only watch it 'cos Leonardo's in it.' Iris let out a loud, swoony sigh. 'Now that man could definitely be 'The One'.'

Elodie laughed. 'In your dreams.'

'Every girl's gotta have a dream. Ooh. I think they might be coming here.'

'Who? Leonardo DiCaprio and Kate Winslet?'

Iris tutted at Elodie. 'Don't be stupid. The lot who nearly drowned. Look.'

Elodie moved closer to the window and peered through the glass and torrential rain. Iris did the same, her face almost touching the pane. She wiped the misty haze, caused by her breath on the glass with the palm of her hand. Marian instinctively handed her a paper serviette to do a better job.

'When did you last clean these windows?'

Iris held the now damp – and decidedly grey – serviette between her finger and thumb before dropping it near the edge of the table. She then returned to her previous position.

Marian scooped up the dirty serviette with another dry one, rolled them into a ball, and dropped it into her apron pocket.

'Just before Christmas.'

She leaned forward, pressing her hands on the edge of the table so that she too, could watch the newcomers.

'I have to tell you,' Iris said, 'that tall, broad-shouldered guy looks pretty hot from here. And blond. Definitely my type of guy. Anyway. He's pointing in this direction.'

Marian couldn't stop the sigh from escaping.

'Yeah. But the equally tall … and it has to be said, equally broad-shouldered, brown-haired girl is pointing towards the pub.' Elodie grinned. 'And no. Before you make any jokes, Marian, she's not my type. Archer's my type.'

Marian, who wasn't feeling in a particularly jokey mood right now, hadn't intended to say anything of the sort, and said so.

Iris' gleeful expression had returned. 'I bet you a sticky bun that they'll come here.'

'They won't,' Marian said, decisively. 'So you're on.'

'Don't they realise it's pouring with rain?' Elodie furrowed her brows. 'What is wrong with them? Are they completely mad? Why're they just standing there?'

Iris shrugged. 'I think they're waiting for the other guy. That man-mountain, who's clearly part orangutang, part beach-bum slash surfer dude, to tie up the tender thingy. Is that what it's called? And I think they may be the crew, not the owners. They don't look particularly well-dressed. From here it looks as if they're all just wearing jeans and waterproof jackets ... Wait. They're moving.'

And then, to Marian's delight, all four of the strangers had hurried up the path from the little jetty that sat midway between her café and Archer's pub, and turned right, not left, at the top of the steep incline.

It only took a couple of minutes for them to arrive at Cove Café and yet when the little bell tinkled as they shoved open the pink front door, Marian jumped at the sound.

'Welcome to Cove Café,' she said, giving a small cough to clear her throat before beaming at them. Iris was right. They weren't that smartly dressed. But their jackets were dripping pools of water onto Marian's floor. She pointed to the coat stand near the door. 'You can hang your coats on that stand, and sit at any table you choose. Other than this one. Because it's occupied.'

What on earth was she babbling about? Why had she patted Elodie and Iris' table and said such a stupid thing?

She heard Iris whistle, and she glanced at her. Iris was staring at the man she had described as hot ... and licking her lips.

Marian shook her head and blinked away the image of Iris leaping across the table and throwing the guy to the floor, but when her own eyes met his, she was instantly tempted to do the same.

A rush of heat, like the one she got whenever she opened the oven door, swept across her face, down her neck, her body, and even to her toes. And, as ridiculous as it might seem, as a crooked smile spread across the undeniably handsome, stranger's mouth, Marian felt her entire body lift somehow. As if her feet were no longer touching the tiled floor. Which, of course, they were. She knew that. But she felt lighter. Taller. Happier. How weird.

'God!' the handsome stranger exclaimed. 'It smells so good in here.'

'It does,' the tall, brown-haired girl agreed, darting a look at the man and snarling just a little. 'Probably because all our senses are so thankful we're not dead, they're heightened ... and having a party.'

'I'm hungry,' the smaller of the two women said. She had purple hair, freckles across her slightly upturned nose, and looked as if she might nod off any second. And just to prove the point, she yawned.

'I'm starving,' added the man-mountain-cum-orangutan-beach-bum-surfer.

'Then you've come to the right place.' Those words had been a trumpet blast to Marian's ears. 'Make yourselves at home and I'll get you the menus. There're some specials on that board.' She nodded in the direction of the large blackboard that hung on one wall beside the main counter; the white, swirly writing, offering delights such as her Breakfast Special Pancakes, amongst others. 'I'm Marian. The owner. If you don't see anything you like, just ask, and I'll see what I can do.'

The handsome stranger, who was looking at her as if he'd definitely seen something he liked … but then suddenly wasn't so sure, glanced from her to the blackboard.

'Breakfast Special Pancakes',' he said, and continued reading out loud. 'Six thick but delightfully light, pancakes, four large rashers of scrumptious bacon, lashings of heavenly maple syrup, and mouth-wateringly creamy scrambled egg on the side. Hmm. I like the sound of that. Mind you, Marian's Mega Breakfast sounds good too.'

The man-mountain took over. 'Everything a full English breakfast should be – and more. It comes with two chunky sausages, two large rashers of scrumptious bacon and two freshly-laid eggs. Plus, tasty tomatoes, or baked beans, or both; a mound of mushrooms – not magic … but you'll think they are!' The man laughed at that part. 'And two slices of toast, white or wholemeal, butter and your choice of homemade marmalade or jams, along with a large mug of refreshing tea or coffee.'

'I think we can guess what you're having, Jasper,' the brown-haired woman said. She still didn't sound very happy.

'How freshly-laid, exactly, are the eggs?' The one with the purple hair asked.

'Umm...' Marian wasn't sure how to respond to that.

'Still warm from the chicken's bum.' Iris stood up, giving a little wave and then she walked towards the group. 'Hi. I'm Iris. That's my best friend, Elodie and that's Marian, the owner, as she's already told you.' She pointed briefly to Elodie and Marian before returning her full attention to the handsome man. 'We watched you arrive. That was really something. We all thought you were going to end up at the bottom of the sea. It looked very hairy out there. Pretty spectacular driving. Or steering. Or whatever you do in a boat. Are you the captain?' She stared up into his eyes.

The man took a tiny, almost imperceptible step back.

'Oh ... er ... yes. And thanks ... I think.'

'Oh, it was something, all right.' The tall woman scowled. 'This death-defying genius is Parker. I'm Belinda. But everyone calls me Bel. The yeti here is Jasper. And the semi-comatose, purple-headed, pea-brained one is Nikki.'

'Hey! I'm awake.' Nikki didn't seem at all concerned about the other remarks Bel had made about her.

'Hello all.' Iris was still smiling at Parker. 'So what brings you to Clementine Cove?'

'A storm,' Bel snapped. 'And that bloody moron.'

Parker sighed. 'Give it a rest, Bel.' He didn't sound angry, just, perhaps, a little fed up. 'You're alive and *The Dream* is safe and sound, so there's no harm done.'

'*The Dream*?' Iris queried. 'You two have a dream? You're a couple?'

Bel's eyes opened wide, as did Parker's.

'Christ no!' Bel said. 'It's the name of the yacht. *The Dream*. But so far it's been more like a bloody nightmare. If one of your life-long friends ever asks you to sail away to the sunny seas of the Med for a summer of fun and frolics – run. Don't walk. In the other direction.'

'That wasn't exactly what I said.' Parker sighed out a breath. 'I said it'd mean hard work, long hours, maybe dealing with some obnoxious people, but also the chance for you and Nikki to possibly meet a few wealthy, single men and that the money would be good and so would the weather.'

'The weather? Ah yes. Remind me. How's that been, Parker?'

'We're not in the Med yet.'

Bel glanced at the specials on the blackboard and her lip curled just a fraction.

'You're telling me.'

'Let's sit by the window,' Nikki said.

The others followed her to the table, after tugging off their waterproofs and handing them to Jasper who hung them all on the coat stand.

Iris hesitated as if unsure whether to follow them or return to her table, but after a second or two, she rejoined Elodie.

Marian wanted to curl up and die. That one brief look from Bel had taken the wind out of her sails.

'I'll get you those menus. And some towels.'

Chapter 6

Parker watched Marian walk away, for just a second, before taking a seat at the table. He had no idea why, but he had been surprised when she had said she was the owner of the café. For some reason, he had assumed she merely worked here and the proprietor was an elderly woman. Or an elderly couple, perhaps. Certainly not an exceedingly pretty woman, with dark brown, almost chocolate-coloured, wavy hair that probably looked even prettier when it wasn't tied into a ponytail. She was around the same age as Bel and Nikki, he would guess; mid-thirties but it was difficult to tell her height. She sort of slouched in on herself, as if she didn't want to be seen, almost. If she held herself upright, she would appear taller, although still several inches shorter than Bel who was five feet nine in bare feet.

Was Marian intimidated by the two women seated at the other window-table? They had seemed like friends when he and his mates had arrived, so he doubted that was the case.

Perhaps she didn't like strangers. But that would be weird for someone who owned a café. And yet there was something about her that looked ... sad. Or worried, maybe? Or unhappy?

Or perhaps she was sick and tired of having to deal with difficult people. Like Bel. Or of running the café. The place wasn't exactly busy. Maybe that was the problem. Lack of customers.

The aromas that had wafted towards him as he had opened the door had been heavenly and he had been genuinely surprised by the interior. From the outside, it was basically a picturesque cottage. You would never guess it was a café until you spotted the sign on the front door, or saw the delicious-looking displays of cakes, buns and rolls on the shelves in one of the other, smaller windows. The ground floor had been converted into a quaint café, no doubt several years ago, judging by the décor. Unless this was meant to be Boho-chic or something.

Shit! Why had he had to think of Boho-chic? Something he recalled Isabella telling him about, months ago. Maybe almost a year. Why had that stuck in his brain? He couldn't even remember why they had been talking about Boho-chic, for God's sake, so why that had popped up right now was beyond him.

He shook his head to try to clear his mind of Isabella, and glanced at the two women at the other table, but he quickly turned away. The one who had introduced herself as Iris was staring at him in a rather odd manner. Almost as if she were planning to murder him or something. Which was a bit bizarre.

'Ow!' He rubbed the red blotch on the back of his hand where Bel had just slapped him. 'What was that for?'

'Because I was talking to you and you were away with the fairies.'

He grinned at that. 'Away with the fairies? Are we five? Sorry. What were you saying?'

Bel sighed and flicked her eyes heavenwards. 'I was saying that I assume we'll be staying here for a while. Until the storm is well and truly over. And I don't mean in this café. I mean in this safe harbour.'

Parker looked at each of his friends in turn.

'Um. Yeah. I guess so. I hadn't thought that far ahead, to be honest. The bay here's not ideal but it'll do. I'll have to check if there are any fees or requirements, but it looked as if it's a natural harbour and I didn't see any signs about moorings, or charges, or who to contact. Did any of you?'

They each shook their heads.

'Nope,' Jasper said. 'Maybe these people know. Or at least the owner of this place. The other two could be here on holiday.'

'Here?' Bel threw him a look of astonishment. 'On holiday? Are you serious? Who in their right minds would come to a place like this for a holiday?'

Parker laughed. 'Don't be such a snob, Bel. Lots of people holiday in the UK. Not everyone is lucky enough to holiday abroad. Not everyone wants to, either.' Bel threw him a doubtful look. 'I thought the bay as we entered was rather pretty.'

She snorted derisively. 'That's because you were grateful we were all alive, as I told you earlier.'

'No, it wasn't. The majestic sweep of the cove, the rugged cliffs, the lighthouse, not to mention the church, surrounded by trees on one side of the mouth of the bay and the bright blue pub with its thatched roof, on the other. It's like something you'd see on a postcard.'

'No, Parker. It's not. No one sends me postcards from ... the 1980s. Which I think I can safely say is the decade this village is stuck in. And the last time this place was decorated. I thought our town was bad enough but Broadlands Bay is at least living in the 21st century.'

'You're being such a bitch today,' Nikki said.

'Tell me I'm wrong. Look around. If you can stay awake long enough.'

Nikki shrugged. 'So the place isn't as on trend as you'd like. Does that matter? Shush. Here comes ... Marian.'

Bel was about to say something more but Parker stopped her with a glare.

'Here're some towels.' Marian handed each of them a plain white hand towel from a pile of four. 'And here're the menus.' She slipped them out from under her arm and placed them on the table. 'As I said, if you don't see what you want on the menu, or on my specials board, just ask.'

'Do you have oysters?' Bel asked without picking up the menu.

'For breakfast?' Marian sounded as surprised as she looked. 'No. But I can probably get you some if that's really what you want. Or ... you can go to the pub. The Bow and Quiver. It's on Arrow Point. Bentley, the chef there, will probably have them. He's a cordon bleu chef, and he really knows his onions. And his oysters.' Her smile lit up her entire face. 'I can call him and ask, if you like.'

'Oh.' Now it was Bel who seemed surprised. 'That won't be necessary. I've gone off the idea. I'll have that mega breakfast thing. But I might go and say hello to ... Bentley, did you say? I too am a cordon bleu chef, trained in Paris. We might know some of the same people.'

Marian raised her brows. 'Isn't that like saying you've got a cousin who lives in some far off place and expecting everyone who goes there to have met them?'

Parker grinned. 'That's exactly what it's like. Bel's in a bit of a mood, so please excuse her rude behaviour. Beneath all the bluster and snide remarks, she's a real sweetheart.'

Bel tutted, blinked and looked away.

'I had a cat like that when I was a kid. It would spit and hiss and claw you to death one minute and then it'd cuddle up against you and purr its heart out the next.'

'Are you calling me a cat?' Bel narrowed her eyes.

'No. Of course not.' Marian smiled sweetly and turned away. 'She was a beautiful cat, and I loved her. I'll give you all a few minutes to decide what you'd like.'

'What the hell is wrong with you today, Bel?' Parker looked her directly in the eye as soon as he thought Marian was out of earshot. 'You're behaving like a spoilt child.'

'And you're being an even bigger bitch than normal,' Nikki added.

'I'd have to agree with what they said.' Jasper's voice always sounded caring when he spoke to Bel. 'What's up, beautiful?'

Bel's expression suggested she might be about to throw a tantrum but instead she took a deep breath and seemed to calm herself. She shook her head and lowered her gaze, dropping her head into her hands and making a sort of growling noise. And then her head shot up and she smiled apologetically.

'You're right. I know you are. I'm sorry. I don't know what's got into me lately. I can't seem to help myself. I've always been ... forthright. Outspoken. Okay. A little bit bitchy. But not in a mean way. Not really. Recently though ... I don't know. What can I say? It's like I've become a different person.'

Parker reached out and took one of her hands in his.

'I may be wrong. And I probably am. And this is really not the time or place to discuss it, but is this ...?' He hesitated. 'Is this as a result of what happened, do you think?'

Bel blinked at him. 'With ... with Morgan, you mean?'

'Y-es. But not just what happened with Morgan. Is it ... is it...?' He still found it difficult to bring up the subject.

'Because I can't have kids? Is that what you're asking? Jesus, Parker. How many times do I have to tell you ... all of you ... that I'm not bothered about that? So I can't have kids. So what? Millions of women can't. It's not just me. Besides, as I no longer have a husband, kids don't really fit into my future anyway. Mind you, I almost didn't have a future today. You nearly killed me. You ...' She stopped, exhaled loudly and raised her eyebrows. 'Sorry. I think we'd better change the subject for now.' After taking a few deep breaths she added, 'I'm definitely having that mega breakfast thing. And I suppose I'd better say sorry to ... Marian, wasn't it?'

'Yep.' Nikki nodded.

'And while I'm at it, an apology to Parker, Jasper and you wouldn't hurt, would it?'

'I might even stay awake for that.'

Bel gave Nikki a playful nudge and in response, Nikki threw her arms around Bel's shoulders.

Bel eased herself away. 'I'm sorry, Nikki. You know I love you really. And you, Parker. I'm sorry. You, Jasper. You, I'm not so sure about. But I'm sorry for being a bitch to you too.'

'That's okay,' Jasper said. 'I love you no matter what. And secretly, you love me too. You're just too scared to admit it.'

'Really? You think so? Hmm. Doubtful, Jasper. Very, very doubtful.'

'We all love you, Bel.' Parker squeezed her hand again. 'And we all know you've had a lot to deal with over the last two years. We forgive you because we know you're trying to sort out your head and your heart. And I know a little bit about how some of that feels. Just remember we're your friends and you can talk to us about anything. Anything at all. Okay?'

Bel smiled. 'Okay. Thanks, you guys. I'll try really hard not to be bitchy for the rest of the day. Tomorrow, of course … well, I'll make no promises about tomorrow. Where is that bloody woman? I'm starving.'

'And you were going to apologise to her for being rude, remember?' Parker said.

'Bugger. I was, wasn't I? Life can be hell sometimes. But at least I didn't drown this morning. So that's a positive, I suppose.'

'Yep.' Nikki nodded. 'The Universe is giving you another chance.'

'It's giving us all another chance.' Bel smiled. 'Believe me, Nikki, I wouldn't have drowned alone. I still don't know how you managed to sleep through it all though.'

Chapter 7

It had been a strange morning. But a good one. Apart from the fact that it was still chucking it down with rain and the winds were so strong that the doors and windows of Cove Café were rattling. That meant Marian was unlikely to welcome many more customers, unless the weather improved dramatically.

Not that there was much chance of that, according to the weather forecast she had just heard on the smart speaker in the café kitchen. Another severe weather warning had been issued and had been upgraded from the amber of earlier to a red.

That was serious stuff. A red warning meant gale force winds that would likely cause damage to garden buildings, fences and even properties. Trees might come down. Heavy rain might lead to flooding in some areas, and there would be disruptions and delays to all forms of transport. It also meant there might be a risk to life.

Mind you, she didn't need a weather warning to tell her conditions outside were pretty grim. She only had to look out of her windows to know that. Elodie and Iris were almost blown along the road when they left just now, as were Marian's other four customers who had returned to their yacht shortly before her friends departed.

Marian was so pleased to have seen Elodie and Iris. They had really cheered her up. And so had her other four customers. Chatting with people her own age always lifted her spirits. In spite of the fact that Marian was jealous of Elodie's relationship with Archer, she still enjoyed El's company.

And Iris never failed to make her laugh. The woman didn't care what she said or did. Although she might've gone a bit too far this morning. Parker, the handsome stranger, had appeared slightly terrified of Iris. Okay, maybe not terrified, exactly, but certainly concerned. Iris couldn't have made it clearer that she fancied the guy, if she had plastered a sign on her forehead saying, 'I think you're hot and I'd like to have sex with you.'

The woman, Bel, had been a bit obnoxious at first. It hadn't really bothered Marian; she was used to dealing with difficult people. But when Bel had had the decency to apologise, that had been a pleasant surprise. Marian couldn't help wondering if Parker had asked Bel to do that. Or maybe it was Nikki, who seemed so laid back it was unreal.

Jasper had seemed nice, too. Marian had the feeling he would be incredibly handsome if he shaved his beard and cut his hair. The man looked like he had recently been rescued from a desert island. Even his clothes were crumpled and creased and his jeans were torn in at least two places.

Parker, on the other hand gave the impression that he paid more attention to the way he dressed – but not too much attention to be seen as vain. His jeans looked ordinary but, once he had removed his jacket, his T-shirt and jumper looked expensive. Not designer, but definitely quality. His watch however, looked incredibly expensive. Marian had never seen a watch quite like it. Overall, the man was handsome and well groomed. The perfect gentleman, as Stella Pinkheart would no doubt call him.

He had certainly behaved like one. He had even offered to help Marian carry the tray from the kitchen doorway to their table because it had looked heavy. Or maybe he was concerned their meals would end up on the floor and he didn't want to wait another ten minutes or so for replacements to be made. Whatever the reason, Marian had been surprised. And pleased. She wished she hadn't blushed quite so much though. But perhaps he hadn't noticed.

Now, she smiled as she wiped down the table where Parker and his friends had sat, and a warm flush travelled over her body. Parker had lovely eyes. Caring eyes. He also had a crooked smile that was oddly sexy. The timbre of his voice was deep and yet gentle. He came across as a thoroughly decent guy. The sort of man you could be friends with as well as a lover. That thought made the heat rise faster. She shook her head and told herself not to be so silly. She would never see the man again. And even if she did, nothing would ever come of it. Bel had said they were all on their way to the Med to spend the summer season there, and after that, Parker had plans to sail to the Caribbean for the winter season and intended to do the same each year for the foreseeable future. They would be leaving as soon as the weather permitted.

Marian had assumed people rich enough to own a luxury motor yacht – which was what Bel had told them *The Dream* was, and that Parker was the owner – would be posh and stand off-ish. Or brash and blingy types who had won the Lottery or something and now dripped gold just to prove they were rich. But Parker was none of those. He hadn't been at all what she, Elodie and Iris had expected when they'd watched the yacht arrive.

Although Iris was right about the man being hot. It wasn't simply that he was handsome and came across as really nice. There was an air of confidence about him that most women would find attractive; but she also got a hint of uncertainty lurking beneath the surface. Marian liked that. Archer was the same. He gave the impression of being tough and totally in control and yet deep down, sometimes Marian was sure he experienced self-doubt and uncertainty.

But she mustn't think about Archer. He was in love with Elodie and that was that.

She bent down and picked up the black rectangular object from the floor. It had been obscured by the plant pot near the window but she realised immediately that it was a mobile phone. As it was at this table, it meant it must belong to either Parker or one of his friends. No one else had sat there today and she had mopped the floor last night and again first thing this morning and the phone definitely wasn't there then.

She flicked open the plain black cover and breathed a sigh of relief. The screen was undamaged and the wallpaper on the locked screen was intact. It was a photo of Parker, taken not too long ago, she guessed, standing between a middle-aged man and woman, with another, older woman, seated front and centre. They had their arms around one another, smiling happily, and Parker, she noticed, held the older woman's bony hand. She assumed they were Parker's family, as the resemblance was uncanny. And as there was no other, younger female in the photo, perhaps that meant Parker was unattached. Or at least, had no one serious in his life.

Marian glanced through the window and could see the yacht rising and falling slowly on the ripples in the bay. She would have to run after them and see if she could catch them before they returned to the yacht. They might be on it already. Not that they'd be going anywhere else until the weather improved. Maybe Parker would realise he'd lost his phone and come back to the café himself. Failing that, she'd have no alternative but to try to get it back to him. She couldn't see anyone around. They must all be back on the yacht.

'Damn it!'

Now she had no other option. But how was she supposed to return the phone to its owner? Apart from the fact it was pouring with rain and blowing a gale, how would she get from the jetty to the yacht? She would need to find a way to get their attention, from the shore.

'This is not how I imagined I'd be spending my day,' she said out loud, as she went to get her coat and boots.

And she took another look at Parker's photo as she did so.

Chapter 8

'Is that person on the jetty waving at us?' Bel asked, peering through the window of the bridge. 'It looks like that woman from the café.'

'Oh God. Really?'

'Yes. Look.'

Parker half expected to see the woman called Iris standing where Bel was pointing, but as he squinted through the river of rain running down the glass, he could see it wasn't her.

'It's Marian!'

'That's what I said.' Bel gave him an odd look. 'You did pay the bill before we left, didn't you?'

Parker tutted. 'You know I did.'

'Well, either she's completely mad – and she did seem a bit strange, especially when you asked her if she knew whether it was okay for us to stay in this harbour – or she wants you to call her.'

'You're being bitchy again. She didn't seem mad to me. A little ... nervous maybe. What makes you think she wants me to call her? Do you think she was attracted to me? I didn't think she was. Not that it matters. I can't get involved with anyone right now. Not for a long time. But she does seem keen to get our attention. You're right about that. Can you hear what she's saying?'

'Are you for real?' Bel slapped his arm. 'Of course, I can't. I don't have super powers, you moron. But I can tell that when a woman is jumping about on a jetty, waving what is clearly a mobile phone and pointing to it and putting it to her ear, she is more than likely asking someone on this boat to call her. And I doubt very much that she's asking me. Or Nikki. And no one in their right mind would want Jasper to call them. But then again, she clearly isn't in her right mind, is she? Jasper!' she yelled, almost deafening Parker. 'I think you may have an admirer. As difficult as I find that to believe.'

Parker stared at Marian. She was looking even more frantic now. Perhaps the woman was a little odd, after all. Bel was right. No one in their right mind would behave in such a way in the middle of a storm. Marian did appear to be indicating

73

that she wanted someone on *The Dream* to call her. She was pointing at the yacht and then to the phone she was waving in her hand.

But how could any of them call her? He hadn't seen her give any of his friends her number.

She was clearly struggling to keep her footing in the increasingly strong wind.

Parker gasped and instinctively moved to help her, but all he could do from where he stood was watch as she stumbled across the width of the jetty, in a crab-like manner, only managing to stop herself from falling into the water by grabbing one of the upright posts lining the wooden structure.

This storm appeared to be building, not blowing itself out as he had expected. He had better check the forecast again to see if it had changed, but first he should ascertain what Marian wanted, and get her safely back indoors.

And he hoped it wasn't that she wanted Jasper to call her.

He quickly dismissed that notion. Why would it matter who she wanted to contact? She meant nothing to him.

Okay. So he had felt an odd jolt when he had stepped inside the café and first seen her. But that was just relief that he was out of the rain. And as Bel had said, probably also that they were all safe and sound and on dry land. Plus, he had really been looking forward to breakfast. Of course, he was relieved. Anyone would have been. And that had definitely been some breakfast. He couldn't recall the last time he had tasted a breakfast as good. Not even one of Bel's breakfasts topped Marian's Mega Breakfast. But he wouldn't tell Bel that.

He wished he had been able to moor *The Dream* at the jetty. Then he could have quickly stepped off the yacht and spoken to Marian. But according to the charts, the water was dangerously shallow there and only suitable for small boats. He had anchored *The Dream* as close as he had dared.

The bay was protected from the currently raging sea by the natural barrier of rocks and only a small channel of water ran into it via the mouth of Clementine Cove. The water there was choppy – and becoming choppier by the minute. He had made sure to avoid that area and had found what he thought was the safest spot. It was sheltered not only by the cliffs but also by the houses, which in turn were shielded by some very large, although madly swaying, trees.

Yet, if the winds grew stronger, and the waves at the mouth of the bay whipped up even more, there was still a chance, however slight, that the yacht may drift on the ripples and slowly be swept towards the rocks at the base of the sandstone cliffs. But if he moved any closer to the shore, he also risked it running aground. It was a catch 22 and there was nothing much else he could do. He had done everything that he could to keep *The Dream* safe and sound.

Right now though, what he needed was for Marian to get safely back indoors. Why was the woman still standing there? She was clinging to the jetty post for dear life.

'Did you see that?' he asked Bel. 'She almost fell into the water just now.' Anxiety was rapidly building in his chest. 'I don't know what she wants but I think I'd better take the tender and find out before she drowns.'

Jasper appeared, a huge smile on his face. 'You called?'

'Did you ask that woman from the café to call you?' Bel asked. 'The owner. Marian. Did you give her your number? Or did you tell her you'd call her?'

'No.' Jasper looked confused. 'Why would I do that? Wait. Are you jealous? Do you think I fancied her or something just because we had some banter?'

Bel looked at him as if he was utterly insane. 'Don't be ridiculous. And just so we're clear. I couldn't give a damn who you fancy.' She darted a look at Parker. 'It must be you, then, Parker.'

'Is that her on the jetty?' Jasper asked, as Parker pulled his jacket back on, and Bel and Jasper peered out at Marian. 'Why is she clinging to that post with one arm and waving at us like a loon with the other?'

'That's what we've been wondering,' Bel said. 'She seems to want one of us to call her.'

'I'll be back as fast as I can.' Parker felt for his phone which he'd left in the pocket. Except he hadn't. Because it wasn't there. He checked the other pocket. Nope. And then he checked the back pockets of his jeans – although he would have felt it if his phone was there. He glanced around and realisation suddenly dawned. 'Shit! That's what she's been trying to tell us. Marian's got my phone!'

Chapter 9

What on earth was wrong with them? Beneath her breath Marian cursed everyone aboard *The Dream*. Breath that was being pummelled out of her by the force of each increasingly strong gust of wind. Couldn't one of them see that she was trying to get their attention? She could make out at least two of them from where she stood and she was pretty certain they had seen her. Why were they just standing there in the cockpit, or bridge, or whatever the place was called, and staring?

She had to admit that she probably looked a little mad. And being blown across the jetty and grabbing one of the uprights to stop herself from falling in the water possibly hadn't helped convince them of her sanity. No one in their right minds would be doing what she was in such atrocious weather. But she was doing it for them, for heaven's sake. For *him*.

Not that he was anything special. She would do as much for anyone. Anyone at all. Although right now she dearly wished she was safe and sound inside Cove Café, watching the boat bobbing about on the choppy ripples in the bay, not clinging to this post for dear life and getting soaked to the skin in the process. Their jackets might have been waterproof; her coat definitely wasn't.

She shivered involuntarily. She'd catch a chill and die. That would be just her luck. At least that would solve her money worries.

She waved her free arm one more time. If they didn't wave back, she would forget it. Parker would realise he had lost his phone sooner or later. Then it would be his turn to battle the elements and come to her to retrieve it. That's what she should've made him do in the first place. That's probably what anyone in their right mind would have done.

Right. That was it. She was going home. She had done her best. As usual, her best just wasn't good enough. She bowed her head away from the yacht to give her face some shelter from the onslaught of the weather. Her eyes stung from being pounded by both the wind and rain, and it felt as if there were miniscule shards of grit or sand scratching at her corneas. She would use some eyedrops to soothe them when she got safely home.

But could she move? She had already nearly been blown into the water by one gust of wind. What if another came just as she let go of this post? The next post was a good three or four feet away and the rope between them, although strong, was swaying wildly. Would it help to hold her steady if she grabbed it?

What choice did she have? She couldn't stand here until the storm blew itself out. Besides, according to the forecast it was only going to get worse, not better, in the coming hours. If she stayed here much longer, not only her but also the jetty might be blown out into the bay and onwards to the English Channel. Who knew where she might eventually make land? Assuming she didn't drown, that is.

Perhaps she could chuck Parker his phone as she floated past his yacht. The image made her smile for a split second.

She wouldn't serenely float past *The Dream*. Not in this wind. She'd more than likely be tossed onto her bum and end up showing everyone her knickers. And she had worn an old and rather washed-out black faded to grey pair today, to match her sombre mood this morning.

But what about the yacht? She certainly wouldn't want to be on that during a red weather warning. Were they aware of that? Were they planning to stay on board? But then again, where else could they go?

She glanced across at *The Dream* one last time, and as the purr of an outboard motor drifted towards her on the wind, she saw the yacht tender speeding in her direction with one person at the helm.

She knew at once that it was Parker, even though his face was hidden by the hood of his waterproof jacket, and it wasn't simply relief that swept through her. It was also something else. Something she wasn't sure she wanted to feel for a man who was only here until this storm blew over.

'Can you grab the line?' he yelled. He tossed it to her with one hand as he manoeuvred the tender against the jetty with the other hand on the wheel.

She wasn't sure she wanted to let go of the post but luckily she managed to catch the line with her free hand and she wrapped it around her wrist and then around the post which she still held onto with her other hand.

Parker leapt from the tender onto the steps of the jetty and was by her side within seconds. He took the line from her and tied it securely to the post. And then, to her surprise, he wrapped one arm around her and pulled her close, while the other held them firm against the jetty post.

'I'm sorry it took me so long to realise what you were saying,' he yelled again. 'You've got my phone?'

She nodded in the affirmative, although she could hardly hear him above the howling wind and the hiss of the rain. The hood of his jacket had come undone and it flapped around his neck and his hair was whipping his face, but she could see the crooked smile now hovering on his lips.

'That's okay,' she yelled back. She retrieved the phone from her pocket where she'd safely stowed it as the wind had made her do her little dance across the jetty. 'I almost dropped it into the sea. Here. Take it.'

'Can you drop it into my top pocket, please?' Rain dripped from his eyelashes and the tip of his perfect nose. 'I don't want to let go of either you or the post, or we may both end up in the sea.'

She was surprised he found it amusing. Although she liked the feel of his arm around her waist and now she wasn't half as cold as she had been. She did as he asked, zipping up his pocket for good measure and for some ridiculous reason, she patted the pocket with the palm of her hand.

'All safe and sound,' she said, smiling up into his eyes.

He held her gaze for just a moment before glancing around them.

'Thanks. This was really good of you, but you need to get out of this weather. I'll help you to the road. Will you be okay from there? I need to get back to the boat and get the tender safely stowed.'

'You're going back!'

His brows furrowed. 'Of course. The others are still on board.'

'Are you sure that's wise?' Her voice was growing hoarse from shouting. 'Wouldn't you all be safer on dry land? They've upped the forecast to a red warning. It's going to get really serious. The last place I would want to be right now is out there on a boat.'

'A red warning, did you say?'

She nodded as her ponytail slapped her cheek. 'Yes. About ten minutes ago.'

He hesitated for a second. 'We should be okay. It's worse here than it is on the yacht. We're pretty sheltered where we're anchored. I was about to check the forecast and then I saw you.'

'They say there'll be thunder and lightning too. I know you don't have a mast or sails or anything, but you're still vulnerable, aren't you? Some small yachts were struck here a couple of years ago and the masts were split to smithereens. Why take the risk?'

He shook his head but his hair was plastered flat now.

'We have nowhere else to go, even if we wanted to. Bel's already checked hotels and B&Bs nearby, just in case.'

'I've got a couple of spare rooms. A double and a single. And a sofa in the sitting room. If two of you don't mind sharing the double, you're welcome to stay with me.'

Why on earth had she suggested that? She certainly had not meant to. It was too late now. Although he didn't seem that keen.

'That's really kind, Marian. But we couldn't impose on you like that. Plus I'm not sure I want to leave *The Dream* to her own devices. Especially if the forecast is for worse to come.'

Marian shrugged. If the man wanted to drown, so be it. She needed to get indoors in the warm and dry. Even with the comfort of Parker's arm around her waist, her teeth were chattering again.

'Okay. The offer's there if you ... change your mind.'

He smiled again and his eyes lit up. 'If I come to my senses, you mean? Thanks. Now let's get you to dry land.'

'I don't think there's any dry land in the country today.'

Marian wasn't sure why she was joking about that. She couldn't recall a storm like this for years. Not even the year the sailboats were struck by lightning.

'Ready?' Parker asked, slipping his arm from her waist and taking her hand tightly in his instead. 'We'll need to make a run for it.'

'Ready.'

She shrieked once or twice, more from exhilaration than fear – because she felt oddly safe with Parker by her side – but she still cringed with embarrassment when they reached the safety of the road.

The wind wasn't as bad here as they were sheltered by the houses but even so, Marian found it hard to maintain her balance.

'I'll come with you to your door,' Parker offered, glancing briefly over his shoulder to where the tender bobbed, twisted and tugged on the line, a little like a large fish trying to free itself from a hook.

Marian shook her head. 'No need. Honestly. I'll be fine from here. I can walk close to the buildings. You get back. And be careful, Parker. Don't forget. If you change your mind, there're beds at my place. And plenty of hot drinks too.'

Their eyes met and held. 'Thanks, Marian.' He gave a small cough. 'Right now, I would kill for a cup of tea. Hopefully, Bel will have the kettle on when I get back. Thanks again for bringing me my phone.'

'Anytime.' She smiled. 'Only next time I think I'll wait for you to come and get it. Not that there's likely to be a next time.' Now it was Marian who coughed. 'Thanks for getting me back here safe and sound. It was lovely to meet you, Parker. And your friends, too. I hope you have a great time in the Med.'

A crease formed between his brows and the smile faded from his lips.

'This sounds odd, I know, but it feels strange to think I won't be seeing you again. I ... I feel as if I know you. As if you are a friend.'

'I know. I ... I feel the same.'

They looked into one another's eyes for what seemed like a long while but was just a matter of seconds.

Parker gave a little laugh and ran a hand through his sodden hair.

'We ... we've just met. And ... the truth is ... I'm still in love with someone else. My ex-girlfriend, Isabella.'

'Oh! Er ... I see. Well, I'm in love with someone else too. A friend.'

'Oh. Well, okay. That's good. I mean ... I'll be in the Med and you'll be here, so...' He shrugged.

'Yes. Exactly. And as you said, we have just met, so...'

'Yes. Yes, we have. Umm...' He shot a look at his yacht and made a sort of gesture like a hitchhiker would, pointing his thumb towards it. 'I'd better go then.'

'Yes. Me too.'

'Bye, Marian.'

'Bye, Parker.'

Neither of them moved, until a loud rumble resounded all around them and a sheet of white lightning lit up the entire sky above the bay.

'Shit! I must go.' His expression was an equal mix of sadness and anxiety.

'Yes, go.' Her smile, she hoped, was one of reassurance. 'Maybe we'll get a chance to say goodbye again before you head off to the Med.'

He walked backwards, as best he could, while being buffeted by the wind. His smile was warm and genuine and he gave her a friendly wave.

'I'll make sure we do. Get home safely, Marian.'

He turned and raced back to the jetty, leaping over large puddles and fighting against the stormy conditions all the way.

'Come back soon, Parker,' she called after him.

But she was thankful that he probably hadn't heard her, and she hurried home as quickly as the weather would allow.

The moment she had closed the café door behind her, and without flipping over the sign from Closed to Open, she ran to one of the tables in the window. Dripping wet from head to toe, she knelt up on a chair. The tender looked much smaller now than it had when she, Iris and Elodie had watched it arrive. It wasn't until Parker was safely back on board *The Dream* and Jasper and the others were helping pull the tender on board, that she finally let out the breath she knew she had been holding.

And then, to her astonishment, Parker stopped, and waved towards the shore. He could not possibly see her from where he stood. Could he? But he clearly knew she was watching. She could only just make him out at this distance, but she knew that he had waved at her, and the squeal that escaped her was one of genuine delight.

Chapter 10

Marian was being completely ridiculous, and she knew it. She had only met the man today and had been in his company for less than an hour. All she knew about him was that he owned *The Dream*. And he was heading to the Med to make shed-loads of money, pandering to a bunch of exceedingly wealthy clients who wanted to spend some time messing about on a luxury motor yacht.

But that *wasn't* all she knew about him, was it?

She also knew he was clearly wealthy enough to own that yacht. And those things weren't cheap. Or maybe he had a massive loan against it. Could you get a mortgage or something similar on a boat? She had no idea.

What she did know for certain was that he was in love with someone else. His ex-girlfriend, had he said? Yes. He definitely had said the word 'ex'. Well, that was good.

Or maybe not.

Another thing she knew about him was that he had been friends with Jasper, Bel and Nikki for some time. She had gathered that from things they had all said when they were eating breakfast.

She also knew, from the photo on his phone, that he took after his parents and his gran in the looks department. But she didn't know if his parents were still married, or divorced. Or if they were alive or ... like hers, sadly not. Or his gran.

Did he live with them when he wasn't sailing his yacht around the Med? Or did he have a place of his own that he called home? Or had he lived with his now ex- girlfriend?

One final thing she knew about him was that for some absurd reason, she was attracted to the man.

How on earth had that happened?

And ... unless she was completely mistaken, he seemed to be a little bit ... just a teensy-tiny bit ... attracted to her.

She stepped out of the shower and wrapped a fluffy, warm from the radiator, towel around her. It was so good to feel human again instead of like some bedraggled urchin. She hadn't realised quite how cold she had been until Parker and his friends had disappeared inside and she'd been left kneeling on the chair watching the yacht bob about on the water in the bay.

She shouldn't really have closed the café to come and take a shower. But in reality, it was very unlikely that she would have any more customers today. The wind was howling even louder than before and the rain lashed the windows as if huge waves had tumbled ashore and crashed against the cottage. She shivered again as if she still stood on that jetty.

Without thinking, she dashed to her bedroom window and peered out. Her heart leapt to her mouth.

Where was *The Dream*?

Panic rose inside her and her heart thumped so loudly she could hear it pounding against her ribs.

But then she finally saw it. Parker must have moved it to what he considered a safer position. The yacht was a little closer to the land but was a bit more sheltered by the cliff. As long as the wind continued to blow in the direction it had been, the yacht should be okay.

She still couldn't help wishing he and the others weren't on it though and as another crack of thunder seemed to make her cottage shudder, she scolded herself for not trying harder to persuade him.

The banging on her front door made her jump.

Was that the wind?

No. That banging was made by a human hand.

Was it him? Had he decided to take her up on her offer, after all?

Marian ran to the hall, remembering just in time that she was only wrapped in a towel. She slid her feet into her slippers, grabbed her dressing gown from the hook on her bedroom door and tied the belt as she raced downstairs.

'I'm coming!' she yelled, a beaming smile on her face as she yanked the front door open. She wanted to throw her arms around him but she managed to retain her self control.

'Hi, Marian. Oh. You're ... umm. Sorry.' He gave an embarrassed laugh. 'Er ... Please don't feel you have to, but if your offer to stay is still valid, we would really like to take you up on it.'

'Of course it is!' She quickly stepped aside, holding the door open as the wind tried to wrench it from her grasp, and freezing rain hit her in the face 'Come in. Sorry about the dressing gown. I've just had a shower.'

'I would kill for a hot shower,' Bel said, giving Marian a grateful smile. 'Thanks for this. It was getting pretty hairy on the yacht. I know you said we were safe, Parker, but right now I'd rather be here than out there.'

'Me too,' said Nikki, yawning. 'I'm so tired I could sleep on this floor.'

'Man, it's grim out there,' Jasper said, his long, saturated hair hanging seaweed like around his weather-tanned face. 'I've spent many days and nights on boats during storms. But this one is a doozy.'

Marian nodded her agreement. 'I've closed the café early. I doubt anyone will be popping out for lunch today.'

Parker smiled at Marian. 'Are you really sure you don't mind us all crashing in on you like this?'

'I don't mind at all. But you'll have to decide who's going to share the double bed tonight.'

'Don't even think about it, you yeti,' Bel said, as Jasper beamed at her. 'Nikki and I will share the double.'

'I'm happy to take the sofa,' Jasper said, looking a little deflated by the put down. 'You can have the single, Parker.'

Parker had obviously discussed the potential accommodation with them prior to their arrival.

'You sure?'

Jasper nodded. 'Yeah. I've spent loads of nights on sofas too. Unless it's one of those cuddle seat things. I'm way too tall for one of those.'

Marian laughed. 'It's not. It's a big, three-seater sofa. And it's in front of a wood burning stove.'

Jasper grinned. 'Sounds like heaven.'

'Follow me then, and I'll get you some towels. You all look a bit like drowned rats. No offence.'

'None taken.' Parker laughed. 'That's exactly what I feel like.'

All four of them followed Marian across the café to the door leading to the stairs.

'There's plenty of hot water so feel free to take a shower or bath. Whichever you prefer. I'll put the kettle on and make us all some tea.'

Chapter 11

'I'm the captain,' Parker explained, as they all drank steaming cups of tea and munched on homemade cakes a short time later. 'Plus the chief engineer, deckhand, sous chef, and bottle washer. Basically, a jack of all trades, if needs be.'

Marian had asked about life on board *The Dream*, and how things would work once they arrived at their chosen destination. She had lit the wood burning stove and her sitting room felt cosy, if, perhaps, a little cramped. Each of them had showered and changed into dry clothes and the atmosphere was relaxed and friendly.

'Jasper's the bosun and main deckhand,' Parker continued. 'Plus like me, he can turn his hand to almost anything. Bel's the chef. She also helps out with whatever might need doing. Nikki's chief steward. Well, the only steward, so we'll all have to help her out when we've got clients on board. Basically, we'll all muck in where needed and do what's got to be done. That includes cleaning the rooms, the windows, the decks. Everything, from top to bottom, inside and out. I'm a dab hand at vacuuming, let me tell you. But I'm not so good at making beds. Nikki can do that with her eyes closed.'

'And she usually does,' quipped Bel.

'What can I say?' Nikki shrugged. 'It's a gift.'

Parker grinned. 'Nikki also sets and dresses the table for the guests. They like to see something special. A theme or something. Nikki's great at that. She also organises all the trips away from the yacht. Day trips to places of interest that the clients might want to see. Or a picnic in a secluded cove. A bit like this one. Only warmer.'

Bel's the only one who can cook though,' Nikki added. 'So she's the star of the show as far as the clients are concerned.'

Bel inclined her head – Queen-like, and gave a smile and a Royal wave.

'When Parker's not trying to drown us,' she said, still smiling, 'He's the real star, as the captain. The yacht won't go anywhere without him.'

'True.' Parker held his head up haughtily, and grinning, stuck out his little finger as he lifted his cup. 'But I don't feel much like a star when I'm cleaning the loos, believe me. That's one thing Bel flatly refuses to do.' He laughed. 'I can't really blame her. If we had a bigger boat and could fit more crew on board, I'd happily never clean another loo for the rest of my days.'

'You wouldn't believe it, Marian,' Bel said. 'But all the clients like to cosy up to the captain. It makes me cringe sometimes. Every woman who comes on board – and some of the men for that matter – sets their sights on the captain. If Parker wanted to, he could get laid every single night.'

'Except I won't,' he said, sounding serious. 'Not only because it's unprofessional to sleep with the clients, but also because I don't want to.'

'Unless they're really hot,' said Nikki.

'No, Nikki. Not even then. We talked about this, remember? No sleeping with any one who has paid to be on board.'

Nikki grinned. 'I know. I was just winding you up.'

Bel, who was sitting beside Nikki on the sofa, gave her a playful shove.

'You're never awake long enough to sleep with anyone. I swear there's something wrong with you. I've never known anyone sleep as much as you.'

As if on cue, Nikki yawned. 'Just because I need a lot of sleep, it doesn't mean there's something wrong with me.'

Parker grinned at her over his cup. 'Perhaps if you didn't spend half the night playing games on your phone, you wouldn't need to sleep during the day.'

'And how would you know how I spend half my night?' Nikki's grin was mischievous.

'Because, as your Lord and Master, I know what all of you get up to.'

'He's probably got those minicams hidden in our bunks,' Jasper joked.

'Eew!' Bel shivered dramatically. 'Just the thought of that makes me cringe. I've watched *Below Deck*, and how those people agree to do that is beyond my comprehension.'

'They get paid,' Jasper said, beaming. 'Probably quite a lot. I'd do it.'

'Why doesn't that surprise me?' Bel rolled her eyes.

'What's *Below Deck*?' Marian had never heard of it.

Bel raised her brows. And her voice. 'Are you for real? It's a reality show filmed on board a luxury yacht. A superyacht, in fact. And it's addictive.'

'I haven't watched it either,' Parker said. 'Even though Bel keeps telling me I should. I'm not really a fan of reality TV. "Life is for living," my dad always says. "Not for watching other people live theirs." And I agree wholeheartedly.'

'Yeah, man,' added Jasper. 'Life's short. We need to make the most of it.'

'Well, we're certainly living the dream, aren't we?' Bel did another eye roll. 'Are we all going to reel off clichéd affirmations?'

'I'm not sure I can think of any.' Nikki looked thoughtful.

'Oh. You're still awake,' teased Bel.

'Bel was once a champion swimmer,' Nikki said, changing the subject completely it seemed. 'She could've competed at Olympic level, if she'd wanted to. But she didn't. Instead, she became a chef. Not to mention, a champion bitch.'

Bel gasped. 'I'm not a ... Okay, I am. And I promised earlier I wouldn't be a bitch again today, didn't I?' She let out a long, dramatic sigh. And then she reached out and took another cake from the plate on the coffee table. 'These cakes are sooooo delicious, Marian. What? I'm not being bitchy, I'm being honest. They are delicious.'

'They are.' Parker glanced at Marian. 'Bel's got a bit of a volatile personality. She'll be the first to admit that.' Bel nodded in agreement as she stuffed the cake into her mouth. 'But she's a great friend and she'll do anything for you, once she gets to know you.'

Bel raised her brows and swallowed hard. 'I don't know about that. If you asked me to go back to *The Dream* before this storm is well and truly over, I'll tell you where you could shove it.'

Jasper stretched his neck and back to look out of the window. 'It's getting worse.'

Parker stood up and went to take a closer look.

'The water in the bay is still relatively calm and the bay is pretty well sheltered. The anchor will hold, I'm sure of that.'

'Yeah,' Jasper said. 'Provided the wind doesn't suddenly change direction and swing her towards those rocks. I know you've checked for that, and there's not much we can do about gusting winds in a storm like this, anyway, other than hope.'

Parker nodded. 'I've set the anchor alarm. Not that that'll help much with me so far away. It's not as if I could get to her fast enough to stop her dragging. Perhaps I should've stayed on board.'

'No way,' Bel said. 'I know how much she means to you, but if she's damaged, she can be repaired. You might not be so lucky. This is the first red weather warning we've had, and we're not taking any chances when life is at risk. Any more chances, I should say, as you nearly killed us getting here.'

'He wanted to stay,' Nikki said. 'We told him we would never sail with him again if he didn't come ashore with us.' She grinned. 'Mind you, if he had stayed, and been killed, we wouldn't be sailing with him again anyway.'

'Thanks,' Parker said. 'At least this bay is only semi-tidal and the water level doesn't actually drop that much when the tide goes out, so we needn't worry about that.'

'How do you know that?' Marian asked. 'I thought you said earlier that you hadn't heard of Clementine Cove until today.'

'I hadn't,' Parker said. 'But our charts tell us everything about we need to know about it.'

'Really? Everything?'

Parker smiled. 'Everything about the terrain and sea conditions, tidal flow, et cetera. Basically, all a sailor needs to know about his – or her – current position. And about what to expect, and any obstacles that might be encountered on the planned voyage.' After another glance outside, he returned to his armchair. 'Before we leave, why don't you come on board and have a look around? We could even take you out for a few hours. Just so that you can see what it's like to sail aboard a motor yacht. Unless you've been on one?'

'No. Never. I'd love that. If you have the time.'

'We'll make time. It's the least I can do to repay you for your kindness. Even I'll admit I'd rather be in here – with you – than out there at the moment. As much as I'm worried about *The Dream.*' A strange sigh escaped him. 'And right now, I don't just mean the yacht.'

Chapter 12

'How long have you all known one another?' Marian asked.

She and Bel were in the kitchen doing the washing up, while Nikki was making up the guest beds.

'It's what I do,' Nikki had said, when Marian had mentioned that she would do that after she had washed up. 'Just show me where the linen is, and I'll have it done in no time. And Bel can help you with the dishes.'

'What can we do?' Parker had asked.

'You could get some more logs for the fire, if you don't mind. I'm afraid they're in the garden shed, so it means you getting wet again. There's an umbrella by the back door. But I don't suppose it'll be much good in this weather.'

'Do they need chopping?' Jasper looked excited. 'I'm good with an axe.'

'Says the guy who looks like a mass murderer.' Bel pulled a face.

Marian laughed and shook her head. 'No. There should be some already chopped.' She saw the disappointment on Jasper's face. 'But there's an axe hanging on the shed wall, and a stack of larger logs at the very back. You could chop those into smaller ones if you really want to.'

'He really wants to,' Parker said, laughing. 'Where's the back door?'

'Usually at the back of the house.' Bel rolled her eyes and glanced at Marian. 'He's not as smart as he looks.'

'I meant, do we need to go via the café, or is there another access?'

Marian got up, picking up the plates, cups and saucers and loading them onto the tray she had left leaning against the coffee table.

'There's a door to the garden from the kitchen up here.'

'I'll take that.' Parker took the tray from her. 'After you.'

'The linen?' Nikki asked, as everyone else followed Marian.

'Oh. It's in the airing cupboard in the hall.' Marian pointed to her left. 'That way. Second door on the right. There are more towels in there too.'

'We don't need fresh towels.' Nikki smiled and turned in the opposite direction to the others.

'That's the door to the garden.' Marian pointed to the half glazed door at one end of the kitchen. 'Be careful. The steps are sometimes slippery when they're wet.'

'If we're not back in half an hour,' Parker said, grinning, 'you'll know Jasper's gone crazy with the axe.'

'Don't joke.' Bel looked deadly serious. 'I've always had my suspicions about the yeti.'

'Aww, Bel! I knew it. You do think of me all the time.' Jasper positively glowed.

'I never think about you unless it's absolutely necessary.' Bel turned her back to him. 'Is this the dishwasher?'

It was obvious it was, but nonetheless, Marian nodded, although she still had one eye on Parker as he and Jasper headed towards the garden shed.

'I don't put these in the dishwasher though. They're porcelain. And they're old, and are not dishwasher safe.'

An amused expression swept over Bel's face. 'I see. You got out the best china to impress us, did you?' She laughed. 'I'd have done the same. And it's really beautiful, so I don't blame you.'

'It was my mum and dad's favourite set.'

'Was?'

Marian nodded. 'They both died when I was in my teens. Dad first. Mum, a couple of years later.'

'Oh God, Marian. I'm so sorry. I had no idea.'

Marian shrugged. 'Why would you? It's fine. It was a long time ago.'

'You never get over losing them, though. Do you?'

'No. Oh. Are yours gone too?'

'No. They're both alive and kicking. Often, one another. I'm joking. Although not entirely. They fight like cats and dogs. I have no idea why they're still married. Sometimes, I think they hate one another. That's one of the reasons I took up sailing. Neither of them likes the water, so it was the perfect way to escape. I could spend all day at sea, and then go home and collapse into bed. I joined the local sailing club when I was eight. My gran worked there, behind the bar, and she got me in for free. I think she was sleeping with the president of the yacht club, but that's another story. Anyway, that's where I met Nikki and Parker. They, along with a few qualified instructors, taught me how to sail. They had both been on boats since they could walk.'

'Wow. And Jasper?'

Bel puffed out an exasperated gasp. 'He joined a few years later.'

'He ... he seems to like you ... a lot.'

Bel rolled her eyes. 'He drives me bloody nuts. He never used to be like this. It's only since...'

'Since when? Did something happen between you two?' Marian couldn't help but smile.

'God no! I'm not completely mad. Although some people might dispute that. Oh hell! I suppose I might as well tell you.' She looked Marian straight in the eye. 'I got married three years ago. To a guy I'd known for years. Not from the sailing club. He lived round the corner and we were always bumping into one another. Then one day he asked me out and ... a few years later we got married. The bastard cheated on me. Not once. Not twice. Three times – that I know of. Nikki, Jasper and Parker kept telling me to leave him. But would I listen? No. You'd think, with parents like mine, I'd have learnt something. It seems not. Anyway. When I told him I thought I was pregnant, he decided he didn't want to be a dad. He ran off and left me, and I have no idea where the hell he is. Not that I care that much.'

'You were pregnant?'

'Oh. Yeah.' She dismissively waved an arm in the air. 'But I had a miscarriage and lost it. Then they discovered I had a tumour in my womb, so I had to have it removed. The tumour and my womb.' She laughed, but it wasn't a cheery sound.

'Oh Bel, no. I'm so sorry. But you're okay?'

'I am now. Yes. But I didn't handle it well. Some people can handle it with dignity. With a sort of calm acceptance. Not me. I screamed. I cried. I had endless tantrums.'

'No one would blame you for that. I can't imagine what it must have felt like.'

'The thing is, I was really lucky. And in a way, the miscarriage helped me, because when they found the cancer, it was in the early stage. So after the hysterectomy, I didn't need chemo. But it does mean, I can't have kids. Not that I had thought about having them. I hadn't. Everyone seems to think that's weird. Anyway. Since all that. That's when Jasper started behaving as if he idolises the ground I walk on. I keep telling him it's not going to happen. But the guy just can't take the hint. I swear, one of these days, I'm really going to lose it.'

Marian wasn't sure how to respond to that.

'Perhaps you need to sit him down and explain how you really feel.'

'I've tried. I'd have more luck explaining it to a brick wall.'

'Have you ... have you tried asking Parker to have a word?'

'What? A man-to-man talk, you mean? The problem is Jasper is like a sponge. You think that what you say to him soaks in, but in fact, all it does is leak out the other side. I'm hoping he'll meet someone when we're in the Med, and they'll fall madly in love with one another. But unless he shaves off that beard, cuts his hair, and generally tidies himself up, that's not going to happen. No woman is going to fall for him the way he looks.'

'I don't know about that. Love is blind, so they say.'

'Yeah. And there's someone for everyone. Let's just hope there's someone out there who likes yetis.'

Chapter 13

Marian couldn't believe the meal that Bel served up that evening. It was as delicious as one of Bentley's dishes in The Bow and Quiver. Maybe even better.

Earlier, when Bel had offered to cook dinner, Marian had tried to talk her out of it.

'You're my guest,' Marian had said, in a light-hearted yet firm manner. 'I don't expect my guests to have to cook.'

'It's what I do,' Bel replied, just as Nikki had done earlier, but Bel said it in a tone that suggested she didn't understand why Marian would want to reject the offer. 'Besides, you've been kind enough to let us stay here, so you need to let me do this. You spend your days cooking for others in your café. Isn't it good to allow someone else to cook for you for once?'

Marian couldn't argue with that. It would be wonderful to have someone cook for her for a change. Stella often had in the past, but Marian could not recall the last time that had happened. Neither could she remember the last time she had been out for a meal. She could just about stretch to a drink at the pub and maybe a bag of crisps if she had had a particularly good day's takings, but a meal at a restaurant was out of the question with her finances in the state they were.

She had been mortified at first by Bel's offer. Her cupboards, fridges and freezers, both in the café kitchen and her own, were stocked with fairly plain and simple food. That's what her customers wanted. They didn't come to Cove Café expecting cordon bleu dishes. And as for what she liked – well, she couldn't afford to indulge in luxuries, so her meals were pretty plain and simple too.

But it was more than that. The ingredients she bought were not exactly the finest. She couldn't stretch her exceedingly tight budget to buy organic meat, or even the best cuts of the non-organic variety. Hers were the cheapest she could get, and she was more than a little embarrassed about that now that Bel was standing in her kitchen.

Marian always checked for quality though. She wouldn't serve anything that was even slightly questionable or past its use by date. Her own fridge contained a couple of 'best before' items that had gone a day or two beyond, but they were still perfectly edible – for her. She wouldn't serve those to her customers and she wouldn't serve them to her guests. Thankfully, she could afford free range eggs and some of the vegetables which were locally grown – all from Jury's Farm.

Marian's sigh of relief was audible when Bel looked inside the fridge, spotted the best before dates and congratulated her for not wasting good food.

'So many people throw away stuff that's absolutely fine just because of a date printed on a packet. It's madness. If it looks okay and smells okay, it *is* okay,' Bel said.

Marian was impressed. Bel had surprised her today in so many ways. She could see now why Parker and the others liked Bel so much. It wasn't just because she was a brilliant chef, it was because, as Parker himself had said earlier, "Beneath all the bluster, there's a woman with a heart of gold." Or something along those lines. Marian couldn't recall his exact words.

Bel definitely had a good heart. Marian had discovered that just by chatting with her today. It had been broken, not just once but several times, and not only by a cheating husband, either. Bel's parents clearly weren't ideal. Her husband certainly wasn't. But on top of that she'd been hit by a debilitating disease, survived it, only to discover she couldn't have kids. She had said she didn't want them – but was that true or just bravado?

Marian could only wonder what that might feel like.

A memory wriggled towards the surface but Marian shoved it firmly back down.

Compared to Bel's, her life had been almost idyllic.

Yes, her own parents had died when she was in her teens, but they had adored her and she knew that. Stella had loved her too, and yet, these days, Marian spent hardly any time with her. She must do something about that. As for the other thing, that was history and best left where it was.

Marian still had a roof over her head and a business of her own, even if she now struggled to make ends meet. If the worst came to the worst, Stella would no doubt take her in. Or maybe even Iris.

Bel, it seemed, had no choice but to run away to sea.

But perhaps Marian was seeing things a little too dramatically.

Bel obviously enjoyed sailing, and she clearly loved to cook. She had been singing along to the radio in the kitchen while she had prepared the two-course meal.

Marian had helped her, taking instructions willingly. She had also joined in with the singing, which had caused her even more embarrassment when she realised Parker was standing in the doorway, watching at one point. He had that crooked smile on his face and he winked at her – and at Bel, of course, when they spotted he was there.

Nikki slept, after making the guests beds ... and doing some tidying up, Marian noticed. Jasper chopped more logs, and then came to the kitchen and irritated Bel so much, that Bel threatened to throw a saucepan at his head if he didn't leave.

'You see,' Bel said. 'Why can't he leave me alone?'

Having now spent almost an entire day with him and with Bel, it was obvious to Marian.

'I think he is in love with you, Bel. Deeply in love with you, I'd guess. Archer looks at Elodie in precisely the same way.'

Bel tutted. 'That's what he says. But I know it isn't true. I've known the guy for years. I do believe he's convinced himself that he may be, but I'm pretty sure that he simply feels sorry for me or something. Because of everything that happened. But that's not love, that's sympathy. And sympathy is the last thing I want from anyone. Besides, he's honestly not my type. I'm not just saying that. I mean it. I'm not attracted to him at all.' Bel tasted the hollandaise sauce she had prepared and handed a spoonful to Marian. 'Who's Archer?'

Bel studied Marian's face with such intensity that Marian's cheeks began to burn. As soon as she had sampled the sauce, she averted her eyes as fast as possible.

'Mmmm. That is divine, Bel.' She gave a small cough. 'Archer's a friend. Someone I've known my entire life. He owns The Bow and Quiver. I'm sure I mentioned him before. Or perhaps it was Bentley I spoke of.'

'It was Bentley. Why are you blushing?'

Marian gasped. 'I'm not!'

Bel grinned. 'You are. Sooooo. You've got the hots for this Archer guy.'

'What? No. Absolutely not.'

Bel's grin grew wider. 'You're not a very good liar, Marian. But he's in love with someone else? Wait. Wasn't one of those women who were here while we had breakfast called Elodie? Was that her? Is she your competition?'

'Yes. And no. I mean. Yes, that was El. But there's no competition, believe me. Archer adores her. Since Elodie arrived, he hardly notices me at all.'

Bel looked her up and down.

'You don't exactly make the most of what you've got, if you don't mind me saying so. You're pretty. You've got a fairly good body, from what I can see of it beneath that baggy jumper and that skirt, neither of which, in all honesty, do you any favours at all. Your hair's great. Or it would be if you wore it down and not in that ponytail.'

'What's wrong with my ponytail? I need to tie my hair back for work.'

Bel laughed. 'You're not at work now, Marian. And you haven't been all afternoon. It was down when you opened the front door, after you got out of the shower. Why did you tie it back up?'

Marian shrugged. 'Habit, I suppose.'

'It's a bad habit. Stop it now.' She reached out and pulled the elasticated scrunchy from Marian's hair.

'Ow!'

'Bloody hell. This is something a five-year-old would wear.' Bel shook her head and ran her fingers through the length of Marian's wavy, chocolate brown hair. 'We need to get you to a hairdresser and have this trimmed and styled. And then we need to get you some new clothes. Unless you have anything in your wardrobe that's a great improvement on this outfit.' She drew her finger up and down in the air in front of Marian.

'I ... I'm a bit short of cash right now,' Marian said, lowering her voice and her head. 'Things have been a little slow for a few months. We were all snowed in over Christmas. The entire village. And then it did nothing but rain in January. And so far, February's been just as bad, especially with this storm. I really can't afford luxuries like hairdressers and new clothes.'

'They're not luxuries,' Bel said. 'They're necessities. But okay. Nikki was a hairdresser, many moons ago. I'm sure she'll be happy to give you a trim. Assuming she can stay awake for long enough. As for the clothes. Hmm. We'll have to work with what we've got then, I suppose.'

'Er. This is really very nice of you, but there truly isn't any point. Archer's known me for years and he sees me as a friend. Nothing more. I didn't even know I loved him until I realised he had fallen completely and utterly in love with Elodie.'

'But has he? Maybe if he sees you in a new light, he'll realise it's you he loves.'

'No.' Marian shook her head vehemently. 'Trust me, he won't. You mean well, I know. But some things just aren't meant to be. It would be like me saying that you will realise you love Jasper.'

'Good God. Are you sure? Because that will definitely *never* happen.'

'Neither will Archer falling in love with me. Once, I hoped he would. But he didn't. I've seen him fall in love twice in all the years I've known him. Once ... a lifetime ago. And sadly that ... didn't work out. And at Christmas. When he met Elodie. He never has, and never will, look at me the way he looked at both of those women.'

'Ah. Okay. That's a shame. And I get what you mean. Take Parker, for example. I've never been in love with him, don't get me wrong. But, like you and Archer, I've known him for years and I've seen him fall in love. Parker's only done it once. With Isabella. And sadly, he's still in love with the bloody woman.'

'Oh. Yes. He mentioned her.'

Bel was clearly surprised. 'Really? He did? When?'

'Er ... when he came to meet me on the jetty. Well, not then. It was after he'd helped me to the road.'

'Why on earth would he talk about Isabella at such a time? What did he say?'

Marian gave a cough. 'I really can't recall.' She cursed herself silently for mentioning it.

'Well, that's just weird. Parker goes out of his way *not* to talk about her.'

'It didn't end well?'

Bel snorted derisively. 'Not unless you think your girlfriend and your best friend getting married three months after she dumps you, is a happy ending.'

'Oh my God! Is that what happened?'

'Yep.'

'Recently?'

'As recently as the Monday just gone. That's why we were in the English Channel in the middle of a bloody storm. Because, despite knowing that the weather was going to be dodgy, to say the least, Parker couldn't bear the thought of being in Broadlands Bay on Monday. That's where we all live. Did I mention that? It's on the Northumberland coast. Anyway. That's why we're here. It's all thanks to Isabella, and Parker's best mate, Greg. The ceremony took place at 2 p.m. on Monday, at Parker's local church, St Benedict's. Parker and Isabella dated for five years. Until she decided she'd rather be with Greg. They got married after only three months. Yet another blow to Parker's pride. And his heart.'

'Five years? That's awful. Why didn't Parker propose? Or were they engaged when they broke up?'

'They weren't engaged. And if you ask me, that was part of the problem. Maybe if he had asked her sooner, she wouldn't have gone off with Greg. But who can say?'

'Was he planning to ask her then?'

Bel nodded. 'Apparently he was. At least he was thinking about it. Parker rarely rushes into anything. He's been planning his new life in the Med since he was just a kid, and it's taken him this long to get here. He did all kinds of jobs, and saved every penny he could, but the only reason we're here now other than because of Isabella and Greg, is because someone Parker knew died two years ago and left him a pretty hefty bequest. Parker bought *The Dream* and spent the last two years doing her up. Something else Isabella wasn't particularly pleased about.'

Marian wanted to hear more, but at that point, Nikki had joined them.

'I'm starving. When will dinner be ready?'

'Your timing is almost perfect,' Bel said. 'In about fifteen minutes.'

'Great. I'll get Parker to open the wine.' Nikki smiled at Marian. 'We brought a bottle or two from *The Dream*.'

'Nikki can set the table,' Bel suggested, 'if you show her where everything is.'

'Oh. Okay. But there's really no need.'

'Of course there is.' Bel grinned. 'We're alive. We should make the most of it.'

'And we've all made a new friend,' Nikki added. 'That's another cause for a toast.'

Chapter 14

Shortly after they had finished dinner, cleared the table and loaded the dishwasher, Nikki went to bed.

'I hope you don't mind,' she checked with Marian. 'I'll be up early tomorrow and I'll cut your hair.'

'You're having your hair cut?' Parker sounded bereft. 'But it's beautiful just the way it is.'

Bel and Nikki exchanged odd glances.

'Just a trim and a tidy up, Parker,' Bel said. 'Which is something you should seriously consider having, Jasper.'

'What's wrong with my hair?' Jasper grumbled.

'Oh, where to start?' Bel shook her head in disbelief.

'I don't mind at all, Nikki,' Marian said. 'Pleasant dreams.'

They all said goodnight to Nikki, who was already on her way to the double bed she was to share with Bel.

'Whose idea was this?' Parker queried, looking somewhat anxious.

'It was mine.' Bel settled herself on the sofa, curling her feet and legs beneath her. 'Don't make a drama out of it. It's just a trim, that's all. And Marian's happy, so that's all that matters.'

'Are you?'

Parker's gorgeous eyes seem to burn into her, and as Marian sat beside Bel, she swallowed hard before she answered.

'Yes. I haven't had my hair done for ages. I can't afford to go to the hairdressers, right now, so Nikki's offer is amazing.'

Parker sat on one of the armchairs, his brows tightly knit, but after a while he shrugged.

'Don't let Bel talk you into having anything done that you don't want to. She's good at convincing people they want something, when, in fact, they don't want it at all.'

'Hey! That's not fair. When have I ever done that?'

Parker's crooked grin finally returned.

'You – and only you – are the reason I own several sweaters I shall never wear. Had my hair dyed black. Bought a motorbike, even though I'd never ridden one at the time. Thankfully, I was able to take it back and get a full refund. Mainly due to my dad knowing the owner of the dealership. Do I need to go on?'

Bel laughed out loud. 'I'd forgotten you dyed your hair black. You should have seen it, Marian. Nikki did it for him. Don't worry. She was only about fourteen at the time and had no hairdressing experience. It was one of those semi-permanent dyes, and unfortunately, it rained that day.' Bel couldn't continue, for laughing.

'I'm glad you still find it so amusing.' Parker narrowed his eyes in mock indignation, his crooked smile tugging at the corners of his mouth. 'It's a day I won't forget.'

A burst of laughter came from Jasper, who was sitting on the floor in spite of the fact there was an empty chair.

'Oh man! Was that the yacht club dance? The one where you got a presentation for yachtsman of the year? And you wore that white suit.'

'Oh yes, the suit. Another thing Bel persuaded me I wanted.' Parker shook his head. 'How was I ever stupid enough to wear that suit that night? In my defence, Marian, I was only just sixteen and I'd had the lead role in my school play, which, oddly enough, was a toned down version of a classic film called, *Saturday Night Fever*'. The hero wears a white suit.

Jasper gave him a thumbs up. 'You were really good in that play.' He glanced at Marian. 'Parker's a great singer and an even better dancer. At least he was back then.' He returned his attention to Parker. 'But at the yacht club presentation, the dye ran in streaks, down the front and the back of that suit. And you didn't have time to change, so you went on stage to get your award, and you looked just like a zebra.'

'Yes. I remember.'

Bel bit her lip but her shoulders shook with laughter until she finally controlled herself.

'Everyone thought you were cool.'

'Yes. I'm sure that's what everyone thought.' Parker smiled at Marian. 'I think I've made my point. Don't let Bel talk you into anything.'

Marian stifled a laugh, but not entirely. 'I won't.'

'Do you remember when I persuaded you to try to ride that tractor?' Bel asked.

And before long, everyone was laughing again, including Marian, as Bel, Parker and Jasper regaled her with yet more stories from their shared past.

'Look at the time,' Bel said, several hours later. 'I can't believe it's midnight. I'd better get to bed or I'll look like death in the morning.'

'You always look gorgeous,' Jasper said.

'Get lost, yeti,' Bel replied, stretching her arms out wide as she stood up.

'Is that really the time?' Marian couldn't believe it was that late either as she stared at the clock on the wall. She also couldn't remember the last time she had laughed as much as she had tonight. Or been as happy. She didn't want the evening to end.

'Time flies when you're having fun,' Parker said, an odd sort of smile replacing his crooked grin as he got to his feet. 'And tonight has definitely been fun.'

'It has,' Marian said, meeting his eyes.

'Are those for me?' Jasper pointed to a pillow, sheet and blankets that sat in a pile beside the sofa where Nikki had left them earlier.

'Yes,' said Marian. 'There're more blankets in the cupboard if you need them.'

'I won't. Not with that.' He nodded to the wood burning stove, the logs still glowing red hot; the wicker basket nearby stacked high with more logs ready to be added to the flames.

'Good night, all,' Bel said, ambling towards the door.

Marian smiled as she and Parker cleared the glasses from the coffee table.

'I can manage,' she assured him.

'It's quicker with two,' he said.

Jasper wished them goodnight as he made his bed on the sofa and they headed to the kitchen.

'It's still blowing a gale out there,' Marian said, suddenly feeling nervous now that she and Parker were alone.

Throughout the evening, Parker had gone to the window to peer out at *The Dream*, the last time being just before Bel mentioned the time, so the comment was redundant, and she knew it.

'Yes.'

Parker placed the glasses he was carrying on the worktop, his fingers brushing hers as she did the same.

'You go to–' she began.

'Marian, I–'

They both laughed nervously as they talked over one another.

Parker took a breath. 'Sorry. You first.'

'Um. I was just going to say that you should go to bed. I'll wash these up.'

Parker furrowed his brows. 'Oh. Er. I ... I was going to say the same.'

The look in his eyes told her that wasn't what he was going to say at all. She dragged her gaze from his.

'It'll take me five seconds. You go. Goodnight.'

She turned on the tap; he reached out and placed his hand on hers. They stared into one another's eyes, his fingers easing hers from the metal and entwining hers with his.

'I ... I'm not sure what's happening.' His soft, low voice made her skin tingle.

'Neither am I.' Her voice sounded croaky, yet almost pleading.

'We'll be leaving as soon as the storm passes.'

She nodded slowly, their eyes still locked. 'I know.'

'I don't do this sort of thing. Ever.' His head moved a little closer, his eyes burned into hers, his fingers tightened on hers as he slid his other arm around her waist and eased her to him.

'Me neither.'

Their breaths mingled long before their lips, which seemed to Marian to take an age to touch, but when they did, the softness of her lips melted into the gentle but firm kiss he gave her. A kiss that quickly grew beyond anything she had imagined. A kiss so deep it felt as if it would never end. As if they had melded into one.

'*Marian.*'

He gasped her name as his hand moved from her waist to her breast, his kisses trailing over her skin from her lips to her neck sending sensations through her that were impossible to deny.

She sucked in a breath and held it as his lips came back to hers.

'Just pretend I'm not here.' Jasper's voice crashed in on them like a cold wave on their hot bodies. But he had already disappeared by the time they broke free of one another.

Embarrassment. Shock. Reality. They all descended on Marian at once. Without another look at Parker, she ran from the kitchen, ignoring his plea to wait, only stopping when she shut the bedroom door behind her and leant against it.

Her heart pounded. Her breathing was too quick for comfort. Her face was flushed; her skin still tingled; her body burned for his.

But this simply could not happen. Not now. Not after Jasper saw them.

She didn't want to be an anecdote; something Parker, Bel, Nikki and Jasper all laughed about when they were in the Med.

'Do you remember that storm when we had to take shelter and that local girl ... what was her name? ... It doesn't matter ... Parker had sex with her ... And we left the following day.'

The soft tapping on her door brought her back to the present.

'Marian? Are you okay?'

She shut her eyes tight and bit her lip, trying desperately to stop herself from yanking the door open and throwing herself in his arms.

'Marian? I'm sorry.'

'Good night,' she managed to say, her back pressed firmly against the door.

'Good night,' he replied, after what felt like an eternity.

She listened as his footsteps moved away, and then she turned, one hand gripping the door knob, one slapped against the door as if one half of her was fighting the other.

She desperately wanted to call his name. To let him in. To make love with him all night.

But the memory of what had happened once, many years before, came flooding back; closer to the surface now; harder to keep buried. Stanley Talbot's file had opened up that invisible wound at Christmas.

Marian still couldn't fathom how he had discovered that secret. Just one of many he had known, it seemed.

And her conversation with Bel today had done the same.

Some wounds never heal completely. Some serve as reminders to take care.

Marian could not go through that again.

Especially not on her own. And she would be on her own. Parker would leave as soon as the storm died down.

Chapter 15

'Morning!' Bel woke Marian with a knock on her bedroom door, and a steaming mug of coffee. 'May I come in?'

'Of course.'

Marian struggled to sit up. Sleep had evaded her all night and she had tossed and turned like the wind chime hanging on the apple tree in her garden.

'Bad night?' Bel's furrowed brow and her slightly scornful look told Marian all she needed to know about her appearance.

'The storm kept me awake.'

'Same here.' Bel placed the mug on the bedside table. 'Nikki, of course, slept like a log. Amazingly, she's up. She'll do your hair whenever you want. I hope you don't mind but I've started preparing breakfast. At least I've got everything out and ready.'

'Oh. Er. No. What time is it?' Marian reached for her phone to check but Bel made that unnecessary.

'It's 7.30. I wasn't sure what time you usually get up, but I thought you might want coffee.'

'Desperately.' Marian smiled, ignored her phone and grabbed the mug of coffee. 'Thanks for this. I'm usually up by now.' She took a sip and glanced at Bel. 'Is ... Parker awake? And Jasper?' She added in a hurry.

'Both up and gone.'

'Gone!' Marian nearly spilt her coffee.

'Don't sound so worried. They'll be back. They've gone to check on *The Dream*. They left about half an hour ago, so they should be back by 8-ish. Plenty of time for you to have a shower, assuming you shower in the morning and not at night. I know some people prefer that.'

'I'm a morning person.' Marian gave her a smile.

'Me too. Anyway, Nikki can do your hair before or after breakfast.'

'And then you'll all be leaving?'

'Er. I'm not sure. The weather's still pretty grim but there's a slight lull at the moment. They forecast another storm though, so we wouldn't get very far if we left. But we'll go if you want us to, of course. Is something up?'

'What? No. Sorry. Still half asleep I suppose. I ... I just thought, when you said he ... they ... had gone ... um...'

'Oh, I see. No. They're definitely coming back. And Parker doesn't seem in a hurry to go anywhere.'

'He doesn't?' Hope rose in Marian's chest.

Bel smiled. 'Not until the storm has completely cleared. He's not going to risk our lives again. Or, more importantly to him, to risk scuppering *The Dream*. Both his boat, and his future, I mean by that.'

'Oh. No, of course not. I understand.'

'Marian, if you need to get some sleep, please don't feel you have to get up just because we're here. We can sort ourselves out. And, if you want, I could even open the café for you. I can soon work out what needs to be done and I won't wreck the place. Or alienate your customers.' She gave a snort of laughter. 'I promise I won't even be a bitch!'

Marian smiled at her. 'That's really kind. But I'll be fine. I'll get up now and have a shower.'

'I'll leave you to it then.'

Marian put the mug on the bedside table and, as soon as Bel had gone, she slid back beneath the covers, and screamed into the pillow she pulled across her face.

Thankfully, the mound of feathers and manmade fibres, silenced her strange behaviour.

She had to get a grip.

The problem was, she had spent the last seven hours or so wondering if she should go to Parker. To jump, naked, into the single bed and make love to him all night.

At one stage, in the early hours of twilight, she actually thought she had done so. But when she woke up sweating, she realised it was just a dream. A wonderful and very realistic dream. So real in fact that her skin still tingled from his imaginary touch; her nipples still hard with arousal; his name still on her lips as she had reached that heady climax. A climax merely in her imagination.

And now it was too late. Morning had dawned and Parker was already up and out.

But at least Parker, and Jasper it seemed, had not mentioned to Bel what had happened in the kitchen last night. If they had, Bel's reaction to her this morning would have been different.

How would Parker behave towards her this morning?

And Jasper? Would he make jokes, or wink at her knowingly?

There was only one way to find out.

Marian's mum always said, 'There's no time like the present. And the present will very soon be the past.'

Marian wasn't sure she was ready for either.

The thought of seeing Parker today filled her with a mixture of excitement and apprehension.

The thought of never seeing him again after he left, filled her with misery and doubt. Doubt bordering on fear. Fear that she might lose something; something she had not had in the first place.

Was she … in love?

Was that even possible?

She had only recently realised she had been in love with Archer for most of her life. Could she fall for someone else so fast? Seeing Archer with Elodie broke her heart. That much she was sure of. Not seeing Parker again, she was almost certain, would make her feel the same.

Lost. Alone. Heartbroken.

Not forgetting, that if things with her business didn't rapidly improve, she would also be unemployed. And homeless.

Life, it had to be said, wasn't looking too promising for her right now.

Bel's mellifluous voice drifted along the hallway although Marian couldn't quite make out the song that Bel, and also Nikki, by the sound of it, were singing. Something to do with sunshine.

'Okay, Marian. That's enough.' She scolded herself as she tossed the pillow to one side and threw the covers off her. 'Time to get up and face the music. Whatever tune today might be playing.'

Chapter 16

Parker was behaving as if last night had not happened.

In one way, Marian was glad of that. In another, she wanted to shout and scream at him.

She decided to go with the first emotion.

She had showered and dressed and, after hearing laughter emanating from the kitchen, and realising Parker and Jasper were there with Bel and Nikki, she had sashayed in to join them.

She had taken more care of her appearance than usual today, even having gone to the extreme of letting her hair hang loose. She had spent almost fifteen minutes trying to make it sit perfectly and not flop over her face.

She had applied mascara – a rarity for her, and lip gloss. She had put earrings on and taken them off. She had changed her dress at least three times, even though her choice of clothes was limited.

She had finally decided on a plain, dark blue dress that she had been told brought out the colour of her eyes. Though who had told her that she could not recall. Probably Stella. Or possibly Archer, on one of those days when he had realised she needed perking up. He always seemed to know when that was what she needed. At least he had done so. Until Elodie had come along.

Dismissing Archer – and El, from her thoughts, she studied her reflection. She had to admit she was pleased. Despite her lack of sleep her eyes looked bright, her complexion smooth, her hair lustrous. The dress showed off her figure.

And yet, after she entered the kitchen, other than a cursory glance followed by a quick double-take, Parker had hardly looked at her.

'Morning,' was all he said.

He hadn't even smiled at her. In fact, if anything, he'd ... frowned.

'Good morning, all!' Was the sing-song quality to her voice a bit too much? So what. She could play him at his own game. 'How are you all today? Did you sleep well? How's *The Dream* this morning? Not a nightmare, I hope.' Her strangled laughter was definitely weird.

Judging by the look everyone but Parker was giving her, they all thought so too. He didn't bother to look up. He continued to study his phone. She almost wished she had dropped the damn thing in the sea yesterday.

'Like a log, thanks,' Nikki said. 'That's bed so comfortable.'

'I slept great.' Jasper gave her a friendly smile. 'That sofa's comfy too. How about you? You look fantastic today.'

'Oh. Thanks.'

Was that a surreptitious glance from Parker? Or just wishful thinking on her part?

Parker cleared his throat, but kept his eyes on his screen. '*The Dream* is still intact. Thankfully. Not as much as a scratch, from what we could see. The weather's not good though. Bel said she mentioned that we probably won't be going anywhere today.' He finally looked up. 'Unless you want us to.'

The look in his eyes took her by surprise, momentarily throwing her off balance. There was a hint of annoyance mixed with admiration. And something else.

'What? No, of course not. You're welcome to stay for as long as you ... want to.'

'Thanks.' He returned his attention to his phone. 'That saves us looking for somewhere else to stay tonight. The storm that's coming is predicted to be as bad as yesterday. It's unusual to get two storms so close together.'

'It's unusual to get one storm, let alone two as severe as these,' Bel added.

'True,' Parker agreed.

'It's Fate,' Nikki said. 'Is breakfast ready?'

'More likely, global warming.' Bel nodded. 'And yes. Breakfast is ready.'

'It smells like heaven,' Jasper said, sniffing the air. 'As do you, Bel.'

'I wish we could say the same about you.' Bel rolled her eyes.

Jasper sniffed his armpits. 'I had a shower. I smell okay.'

'Okay is not the same, nor anywhere near, heavenly. You should wear aftershave, like Parker always does. Oh, wait though. You'd have to *shave*!' Bel emphasised the word.

'That's it.' Jasper raised himself to his full height. 'Nikki. When you've done whatever it is you're going to do with Marian's hair, will you cut mine? And my beard.'

Everyone in the room fell silent.

'Are you sure?' Parker asked, after a second or two, looking at Jasper as if the man had lost his mind, not simply requested a haircut and beard trim. 'Bel can talk you into anything, remember.'

'Yeah,' said Nikki. 'If you're sure that's what you want.'

'Don't do this for me.' Bel sounded unsure of herself now. 'It won't change anything between us. Beard or no beard, I'm not interested.'

Jasper shrugged. 'A change might do me good. I was thinking of cutting it all off in the summer anyway. A few months early won't make much difference.'

'I think you'll look very handsome,' Marian said.

The look Parker shot at her didn't go unnoticed and she smiled inwardly. Her happiness didn't last long.

'I'm going back to *The Dream* right after breakfast,' he said. 'I may as well get as much done as I can before the next storm hits.'

'What have you got to do?' Marian asked, without realising she had said the words out loud.

'There's always something to do on a boat. And you've got a business to run. I don't want to get in your way.'

She was going to say he would never get in her way, but she thought better of it. She had a feeling there was more to his statement than he'd said, and it wasn't just about today.

Was he reminding her that their lives were on completely different paths?

Although, unless her business affairs picked up she had no idea where her path might lead in the future.

She had assumed, since opening Cove Café, that she would run the business for most of her life. She hoped that marriage ... and if she was lucky, kids, would come along at some stage, but the café would still be there.

She had grown up in this cottage; her parents had lived here. How could she possibly leave the place?

She might not have a choice.

She dismissed that awful notion.

She would find a way to keep Cove Café going, no matter what it took.

Since turning thirty-five last year, she had wondered what it would be like to run the business on her own for the rest of her days. You were never too old to meet someone, she knew that, but the more the years slipped by, the pendulum swinging constantly from one year to the next, the prospect of finding 'The One' moved farther into the distance.

And then, at Christmas, she had received that file.

The bullet points on the first page had shocked her to the core. Not only was each one of them a secret she had kept, or so she had believed, each one of them was true.

The final one had taken her a while to admit to, saying as it did:

- 'She's in love with Archer Rhodes. And has been most of her life.'

She had asked herself that question many times over the years but had always decided they were merely friends who loved one another as such.

But she had definitely felt jealous when she had first seen Elodie and Archer kissing. And every time after that, whenever she saw them showing affection towards one another – which with those two was every time they were together.

Once she had seen that file, she thought more seriously about it. Was she in love with Archer?

After further bouts of jealousy – because the couple couldn't keep their hands off one another, she reluctantly conceded that Stanley Talbot, deceased, was correct.

But how did she feel right now? Today?

Watching that crooked smile creep back onto Parker's gorgeous mouth, and his eyes sparkle as Bel quipped that he was always in someone's way and she was surprised he hadn't been thrown overboard several times by now, Marian's slightly melancholy mood seemed to lift.

And when he shot a quick look in her direction, with that smile firmly in place, her heart soared.

Yes. It was true. She had been in love with Archer Rhodes for the majority of her life – so far. But that didn't necessarily mean she would be in the future. In fact, as foolish as it might be, she had a feeling that she was rapidly falling in love with someone else entirely.

Someone by the name of Parker Sanderson.

And that, of course, brought a whole new set of problems.

As if she didn't have enough already.

Oh, well. What were two of her mum's favourite sayings?

'Everything happens for a reason,' and 'Ask the Universe and it will provide.'

Perhaps meeting Parker had happened for a reason. And the Universe had provided a storm to bring him here. Another storm was on its way and that was keeping him here. For now.

What had her mum told her on that final day? Marian remembered it word for word.

"I hope one day you'll find a man you will love as much as I have loved your dad, and who will love you as much as your dad has loved me. And when you find him, darling, don't ever let him go."

Marian might be wrong. It wouldn't be the first time. Her love life had been a total disaster until now. Yet standing in her kitchen watching Parker study his phone, his eyelids lifting every now and then to sneak a glance in her direction, she had to ask herself the question.

Could Parker be 'The One' for her? And, equally important, could she be 'The One' for him?

She was pretty certain she could get over Archer. The problem was, could Parker get over Isabella, his ex-girlfriend? He had faced a storm rather than stick around and watch her marry his best friend. Former best friend, now of course. Would out of sight be out of mind? Or had Parker left his heart and Marian's hope for a brighter future, back in his hometown of Broadlands Bay, with Isabella?

Chapter 17

'You look even prettier than you did.' Bel walked to one side of Marian and then to the other. 'Yep. The haircut definitely suits you.'

Marian looked at the locks of wavy, chocolate-coloured hair surrounding the chair on which she sat, and felt as if they were limbs that had been severed. She swallowed hard.

Before Parker had left, after they had eaten breakfast and cleared up, he had reminded Marian not to let Bel talk her into having anything done to her hair that she didn't want done.

'Remember my zebra-look at the yacht club presentation,' he had joked.

'It's just a trim,' Marian had said, pleased that Parker had finally spoken more than a few words to her. During breakfast they had all talked and laughed about all sorts of things but Parker, once again, seemed intent on avoiding looking directly at her.

Now, his eyes had scanned her hair, and her body, and she had seen a look of something akin to ... longing. The thought had made her heart skip several beats.

'You're beautiful, Marian. I mean ... you have beautiful hair.'

'Thank you, Parker. But isn't what's on the inside more important?' She had no idea why she had said that.

'Yes,' he said. 'It is. And I suspect you're beautiful on the inside too.'

His words sent a thrill through her. She thought he was going to say more on the subject but he smiled, took a deep breath and simply added: 'I'm off to *The Dream*. Jasper's got my number if you need me. Have fun. I'll see you all later.'

Now, sitting on this chair, she hoped he wouldn't be disappointed when he saw her later. And she hoped he would still think she was beautiful. Or at least, that her hair and her insides were.

'May I see?'

'It does look fantastic,' Nikki said, her smile indicating she meant it. 'I know you only wanted a trim, and Bel talked both of us into this, but she was right. The bob frames your face and your eyes look so much bigger. In a totally good way. Not like one of those goldfish with bulging, golf ball sized beamers.'

'I'm always right,' said Bel, rather smugly.

Nikki handed Marian the silver edged, handheld mirror that Marian had brought down to the kitchen. It had belonged to her mum and was one of Marian's most treasured possessions. Her hand shook a fraction as she held it up to see. The gasp she gave was part shock, part wonder, and part euphoria.

She looked so different. Her entire face seemed ... brighter, slimmer, gorgeous. She looked gorgeous. At least she thought so. Jasper clearly thought so too. He strolled into the kitchen, stopped dead in his tracks and let out the loudest whistle.

'Man! You're going to break hearts, Marian. Wait till Parker sees you. He won't be able to control himself.'

Bel and Nikki exchanged confused glances; Marian blushed from head to toe.

'Oops. I don't suppose I should've said that.' Jasper looked suitably contrite.

'Said what?' Bel asked. 'What's going on? Why won't Parker be able to...? Oh. My. God! You have got to be kidding me.'

'What?' Nikki asked. 'What's happened?'

'Nothing happened!' Marian squealed.

'I don't know about that,' Jasper said, putting his foot in it again. 'It looked to me as if something was definitely happening last night. That kiss looked hot from where I was standing.'

'Kiss?' Nikki still seemed confused. 'What kiss? Who kissed ... Ooooh! You didn't?' She stared at Marian for a second or two and then hooted loudly, raised both arms in the air and did an odd sort of dance around the kitchen table. 'Whoop! Whoop! Good for you, Marian. And bloody good for Parker.'

'Whoop, whoop indeed.' Bel's dry tone didn't sound anywhere near as enthusiastic. 'It's none of our business, naturally, but was this just a quick hook up, or are you hoping for something more? Only, I hate to point this out, but you own a café here and Parker's on his way to the Mediterranean.'

'Without us?' Nikki shrieked.

Bel tutted. 'I didn't mean he's on his way right now, you idiot.'

'Phew. I thought it was odd he hadn't said goodbye. Not that he could really leave without us. And he wouldn't.'

'Oh shut up and go back to sleep.' Bel sighed. 'I thought there was ... an atmosphere this morning. Didn't things go well? Or were you both trying to keep your distance so we wouldn't find out? And as for you, you yeti, why didn't you say something sooner?'

'He asked me not to,' Jasper said. 'But I think he really likes her.'

'He does?' Marian wanted to hear more. 'Did he say that?'

Jasper shook his head. 'Nope. He said he didn't know why the hell relationships had to be so bloody complicated.'

'Oh.' Jasper had well and truly burst Marian's bubble of joy, but a flicker of hope rose to the surface. 'He used the word 'relationship'?'

Jasper nodded. 'I think so. Yep. He did.'

'Again,' Bel said, 'not wishing to pour cold water on this little fire, as long-distance relationships go, Clementine Cove to the Med is pretty far. And is Parker even ready for another relationship? You may just be the rebound, Marian. And no one wants to be that.'

'Bel!' Nikki snapped. 'You're being a bitch again.'

'Sorry.' Bel sounded sincere. 'I'm not trying to be. I'm simply pointing out a few issues.'

'Issues that don't really concern us,' Nikki said. 'It's up to Parker and Marian.'

'It was just a kiss,' Marian said. 'A late night kiss after we'd both had several glasses of wine. Perhaps we're all getting ahead of ourselves.'

'Are you saying you're not interested in him?' Bel asked.

Marian coughed. 'I'm not saying that. But I do realise that he'll be leaving as soon as the weather clears.'

'You could come with us,' Jasper said. 'There's a double in Parker's cabin. Ow. What was that for?' He looked at Bel who had just slapped him.

'That's for being a moron.' She smiled sweetly at Marian. 'Look. I think you're lovely and I believe we could be friends. Good friends. All of us. But being on a boat like *The Dream* is completely different to being on dry land. You have no privacy, to start with. The clients are either morons, creeps, pompous gits, or all three. They're rarely easy going and they are rarely fun to be around. Running a café isn't like running a yacht.'

'You're worried she'll take your job?' Nikki asked.

Bel tutted. 'Don't be stupid. Parker needs this to work. I'm a cordon bleu chef. No offence, Marian, but I'm not sure you could serve the dishes the clients expect. If anyone's job is at risk, Nikki, it's yours.'

'You're welcome to it, Marian.' Nikki laughed. 'Although I do love crewing with

Parker and I've waited to crew on *The Dream* ever since he bought it. But there are plenty of yachts in the Med and they're always looking for stewards.'

'Hold on!' Marian stood up, shaking the loose hair from the towel wrapped around her shoulders. 'I'm not planning on taking anyone's job. I'm not planning on going to the Med. I'm not planning anything. And Parker hasn't mentioned it either. It was just a kiss. One kiss. We didn't sleep together. We didn't plan to kiss one another again. We might not. I don't know. I really think we should forget this whole thing right now. And please don't say anything to Parker. It was awkward enough this morning. Let's not make things worse. We've got to spend another night together. And I mean all of us, not me and Parker.'

Bel, Nikki and Jasper exchanged looks.

'Fine,' Bel said.

'I can keep a secret,' said Nikki.

Jasper smiled. 'I won't mention it again.'

Bel grabbed Marian's arm and pulled her to one side, lowering her voice. 'I thought you said you were in love with your friend?'

'Oh. Yes. I am. Or I was. I don't know now,' Marian whispered back.

'Nikki,' Jasper said. 'Make me as gorgeous as you've made Marian and then

Bel will fall in love with me. Even though I think she has already.'

Bel tutted loudly. 'Oh, for God's sake, you total and utter moron. I. Am. Not! And I never will be.'

Chapter 18

Marian swished her new hairdo from side to side, like one of those models in a shampoo ad. But she had never seen one of them wiping down café tables. She wondered why she had bothered. Or why she had even turned the sign on the door of Cove Café to Open in the first place. She had been here for almost an hour and not one person had set foot over the threshold.

Compared to yesterday, the weather was not that bad, but it certainly was not a day to be out for a stroll. Or to stop at the café for a drink and to admire the view.

Although that was what Marian herself was doing. Not exactly admiring, more like staring, hopefully.

And the view was of *The Dream* as it bobbed gently on the slate grey waters in the bay. She had seen Parker from time to time, going about his business and doing whatever he was doing on board. From her vantage point, he resembled a toy because he looked so small in the distance, but she knew it was him. Not just because of his physique, but because Jasper was still upstairs in her kitchen being groomed by Nikki. It seemed to be taking forever. But then Jasper did have a lot of hair. And a beard to match.

Once or twice, Marian had waved at Parker, but he had not waved back. He probably couldn't see her as clearly as she could see him. The café windows were not that large and there were no open areas like there were on the deck of the yacht. And yet yesterday, after he had retrieved his phone, he had definitely waved at her.

He had not said how long he would be, or whether he would return for lunch and despite telling herself not to, Marian kept checking the clock. She even checked that it was still working because she was convinced the hands had not moved since she had last looked. But when she put her ear close to the face she could hear the tick-tock-tick so the battery was fine.

Through sheer boredom, she turned the sign to Closed, despite leaving the door unlocked, and ran upstairs. Bel stood outside the kitchen, her arms folded as she leant against the frame of the door.

'Why are you out here?' Marian asked. 'And why is the kitchen door shut?'

Bel made a face. 'He threw me out! Can you believe that? And Nikki didn't try to stop him. They must've propped a chair against the door because I can't get the damn thing open. And believe me I've tried.'

Marian tried to stifle a grin. 'Did you … offer advice?'

'Of course. And they really should've listened. I dread to think what he'll end up looking like. Mind you, anything is better than a yeti.'

'Does it matter what he looks like? I mean, if you're not interested in him anyway, why do you care?'

Bel frowned. 'Because he's my friend. Just because I don't find him in the least bit attractive, it doesn't mean I don't want someone else to. Nikki's great. She's done a fantastic job on you. But Jasper's a huge hunk of a man and what he doesn't need is one of those ponytails while the rest of his head is shaved. Or one of those weird cuts where one side is longer than the other. That looks great on a woman but on a man it's an absolutely no-no in my book.'

'Nikki wouldn't do that, would she?'

'She would if he told her that was what he wanted. And he did.' Bel shook her head. 'He's had that long, bushy hair and that shaggy beard for so many years that I'd forgotten what he looked like when we all first met him. We were in our early teens, I think, when he joined the club, although Parker already knew him. They went to school together. Even then, Jasper's hair was on the bushy side. He wore it in a ponytail if my memory serves me right. I've always known the guy was mad but I didn't realise he was completely and utterly insane.'

Marian shrugged. She was surprised Jasper would like those types of hairstyles, but each to his own.

'It is his hair, Bel. If he wants a style like that it's really up to him.'

'Yes but–'

'Ta dah!' Nikki swung open the kitchen door and stood aside, one arm raised in the air and the other pointing towards Jasper.

Marian couldn't speak. And neither could Bel. A pile of hair the size of a suitcase sat on the kitchen floor.

In place of the mass of yeti-like fur, for want of a better way to describe it, Marian saw a strong, thickset neck, a chiseled jaw with the tiniest hint of stubble remaining, and to her amazement, a dimple right in the centre. Jasper also had well-defined cheek bones, a mouth that looked decidedly kissable, and even his eyes looked bigger, brighter and dancing with mischief and sex appeal. He wouldn't look out of place on the cover of a glossy magazine, and women would be posting memes of him on social media and swooning over his good looks. His now lustrous hair was cut to just below his ears and curled out slightly, giving him an air of youth and a playful quality. Yet it also oozed sensuality, or at least it did to Marian. He wore his new style in a parting, the short sides brushed back from his face but the longer fringe flopped, sexily across his temple. Clearly, like retaining the stubble, he couldn't bear to get rid of the entirety of his former long-haired look. But now his appearance was smooth and sleek, not wild and unkempt.

'What d'you think?' Jasper beamed at them.

'I think women will be queuing at your door,' Marian said. 'I knew you'd be handsome beneath all that hair but I didn't expect you to be drop dead gorgeous.'

'Drop dead gorgeous? I don't think anyone's ever called me that before. Parker, yes. Me, no way. Thanks, Marian. What about you, Bel?'

Bel shook her head. 'I ... I don't know what to think. I'm really glad you went with a normal haircut and not one of the ones you suggested but I can hardly believe it's you. You look amazing. A bit like the guy who plays *Thor*. Only better. And I didn't think that was possible. No!' She held up her hand as Jasper took a step forward. 'Stop right there. I do think you look incredible, Jasper, I really do. In all the years I've known you, I've never seen you look this good. But it still doesn't mean I'm attracted to you. I'm sorry. But there it is. At least now you'll have a chance with a lot of other women.'

Jasper's face fell. But a moment later he was smiling once again.

'I was winding you up with those hairstyles, just for a bit of fun. I knew I was going for a plain and simple look. It's just going to take you a bit of time to get used to the new me. I couldn't believe it either when I looked in the mirror.'

'There's nothing plain and simple about it,' Nikki said, sounding a tiny bit insulted. 'It took skill to get that look. Not to mention over an hour of my time.'

Jasper threw an arm around her and hugged her close to his side.

'You're the best, Nikki. I'll find a way to repay you.'

'The fact that you're happy is more than enough,' Nikki assured him.

She had obviously refused to accept any money from him. She had done the same with Marian.

'Jasper!' Parker stood at the end of the hall, open-mouthed. 'Is that you?' He laughed. 'I didn't recognise you for a minute there. Nikki is a genius. You look completely different. All the female clients will be chasing you around the deck.'

'Thanks, man. I like it too. Bel's still in shock, but she'll come round.'

Bel let out a small sigh and rolled her eyes.

'Marian?' Parker's gaze rested on her. 'Wow. You look ... amazing. I was wrong. I thought you shouldn't have your hair cut, but it really suits you. You look even more incredible.'

Colour rushed to her cheeks and she beamed at him.

'Thank you, Parker. It's made me feel incredible. But the star here is Nikki. She's turned two okay-looking people into the best that they can look.'

'It's surprising what a haircut can do,' Nikki said, smiling proudly. 'I'd forgotten how good it feels to transform someone with just a few snips of the scissors. Although in Jasper's case, I could've used a pair of shears. Maybe I should forget being a steward and return to being a hairdresser.'

'Er. No,' Parker said, his tone half serious, half joking. 'I need you on *The Dream*. Let's not go making any hasty decisions. Decisions we might regret sooner rather than later.'

Had Marian imagined it, or had Parker pointedly looked at her when he'd said that last part?

'Marian?' A male voice called up from downstairs and Marian recognised it immediately.

'Archer!' She shot a look at Parker and the others. 'Excuse me. That's … a friend.'

She dashed along the hall and Parker stepped aside to let her pass, although he did seem to hesitate for a nanosecond.

'Archer?' Bel repeated. 'Isn't he the guy…?'

Marian didn't hear the rest as she raced towards the café, but she hoped and prayed she wouldn't live to regret whatever it was Bel said. If only she and Bel hadn't had that conversation about Archer and Elodie last night as Bel was cooking dinner. Too late to worry about it now. Besides, everyone currently thought there was something going on between Marian and Parker, so maybe Bel would just say that Archer was merely a friend.

But if that was really all he was, why was Marian in such a hurry to get to see him? She nearly fell down the stairs in her haste.

Chapter 19

'Marian?' Archer sounded as if he didn't recognise her as she ran down the stairs towards him. 'You've left the Closed sign on the door but I knew you must be open so I let myself in. Is that you? You ... you look ... different.'

'Different good? Or different bad?' she joked, trying to ignore the variety of emotions tumbling around inside her at that moment.

'Good! Really good.'

His eyes travelled the length of her body and back again as she met him at the foot of the stairs. The look of appreciation, mingled with astonishment, was clear.

'Thanks. Nikki did my hair for me this morning and it's made such a difference. I feel ... like a new woman.'

'You look like a new woman.' He beamed at her for a moment but then he furrowed his brows. 'Nikki? Who's Nikki?'

'Oh, of course. You don't know. Um. She's one of the people from the yacht.'

'The yacht?' He turned his head to glance out of the window. 'You mean that massive, luxury motor yacht moored at the foot of the cliffs near my pub?'

Marian laughed. 'That's the one. She's called *The Dream*, and they're here because of the storm. Didn't Elodie tell you? She and Iris were in here yesterday when they all came in for breakfast.'

Archer looked thoughtful. 'I think she did mention something about seeing a yacht crew in here yesterday. I do remember her saying that Iris was flirting with one of them. As if that was news.' He shook his head and laughed.

'I hope Bentley didn't hear.'

'He didn't. But he was around later when Iris suggested we should somehow try to get in touch with the people on the yacht last night and offer them somewhere to stay. Namely, her place.' He raised his brows in a humorous manner. 'She said she was concerned at the thought of them spending the night on board during a storm, but I think you and I can both agree she had an entirely different reason. Bentley put paid to her idea by telling her he'd seen them all come ashore much earlier and that the yacht's tender was stowed under cover in one of the rock caves in the cliffs.'

'So that's where they put it.' Marian hadn't thought to ask. 'Yes. That's why Nikki was cutting my hair this morning. They stayed with me last night.'

'With you?' He was obviously surprised.

'Yes.'

'Was that wise? How many of them were there?'

'Four. And don't look at me like that. They're all lovely. They're all around our age, too. Mid to late thirties. Parker's the owner and the captain. Jasper's called the boson, but he helps out with everything. As they all do, apparently. Bel – that's Belinda but she likes to be called Bel, is the chef, and Nikki is the chief steward. Well, the only steward. She also gives a hand with anything that needs to be done.'

'You've only got three bedrooms, including your own. Where did everyone sleep?'

'Bel and Nikki shared the double guest bed, Parker had the single, and Jasper slept on the sofa.'

'I could've put a couple of them up. You should've called me.' He grinned. 'Or Iris. She would've loved that. Are they still here?'

Marian nodded. 'They're all upstairs. They're staying again tonight.'

'Because of the other storm that's forecast?'

'Yes. They're staying until the weather clears.'

'Well if the one who slept on the sofa would prefer a bed tonight, just give me a call.' He laughed. 'Or Iris, if it's the guy she was flirting with.'

Marian experienced a sudden stab of jealousy at the thought of Parker spending the night at Clementine Cottage with Iris. She shook her head decisively.

'It wasn't. Iris fancied Parker, not Jasper. But if she saw Jasper today, she might change her mind.' That thought made her smile. 'Nikki also cut Jasper's hair just now. And shaved his bushy beard. If you think I look different, you should've seen what Jasper looked like yesterday, compared to the way he looks today. The guy is positively gorgeous.'

Archer smiled. 'You sound as though you're attracted to him yourself.'

'Me? No. Not to him.'

'But maybe to the other one? Parker, did you say his name was?'

The colour rushed to Marian's cheeks.

'He's nice. They all are. But the minute the storm's gone, they'll be gone too. They

165

were on their way to spend the season in the Mediterranean, giving wealthy clients a dream holiday on a luxury yacht. They only came to Clementine Cove to take shelter from the weather.'

'Yeah. That's what Bentley told Iris. I think he had an inkling she was more than a little interested in the people on board. And maybe one of them in particular. I don't know what's going on with those two. One minute they're together, the next they're not.'

'I don't think Iris sees Bentley as 'The One'. She definitely likes him. She likes him a lot. But I don't think it will ever be anything serious. Not like ... you and Elodie.'

Archer's entire face lit up at the mention of her name.

'I still can't believe we're a couple sometimes. I look at El and wonder how I got so lucky. And it all happened so fast. I fell head over heels in love with her the first time I saw her. It was in here, remember?'

'How could I possibly forget?'

He gave her an odd look. 'You like her, don't you? You're friends, aren't you?'

'Yes!' Marian realised she hadn't sounded pleased about that memory. Which of course she wasn't. But she didn't want Archer to know that. Besides, he was a friend. A good friend. He deserved to be happy. 'Sorry. I didn't mean to sound as if I resent her or something. I really like her. And I'm genuinely pleased you're both so happy.' She gave a little laugh. 'I didn't get much sleep last night, that's all.'

He looked relieved.

'I expect the storm kept a lot of people awake. At one point during the night, El woke me up because she thought the roof of the pub had come off. Thankfully, it hadn't. But we were awake half the night too. You and I both grew up with the noises the wind makes as it whips around the bay, rattles the windows and the timbers, and whistles through the trees, but El's still getting used to it. Although last night was something else. I don't think I remember a storm like it. And they say this next one is going to be about the same.'

'Yes. That's what they say.'

Archer frowned. 'And why do you look so pleased about that? I thought you said it kept you awake.'

Marian coughed. 'Um. It did. Sort of. It wasn't so much the weather that kept me awake, but other things.'

'Other things? Like what?'

'Um. I've got a few things on my mind.' She cast her eyes downwards.

'What sort of things? Anything I can help with? You know you only have to ask.'

Marian nodded, her eyes still gazing at the floor. 'I know. And thanks. That means a lot.'

'Marian? Is everything okay?' His concern was evident in his voice. 'Is there something you're not telling me?'

She shrugged. 'Everything's fine.'

'Is it?' He moved closer, placing his hands on her shoulders. 'Marian, look at me. I've known you all your life. I can see when there's something wrong. And, although it looks fantastic, your new hair style sort of confirms it. Women who've had the same hairstyle all their lives don't often suddenly change it without a reason. What is it, Marian? You know you can tell me anything.'

She slowly raised her eyes to his. 'Um. Business is slow, that's all.'

He studied her in silence. 'That's not all, is it? I've thought for weeks there's been something on your mind but I was so caught up with all the good things going on in my own life, that I didn't stop to ask. And, if I'm honest, I assumed you'd tell me in your own good time. But perhaps I should've asked sooner. Is this anything to do with the file Stanley Talbot sent you? You told me it just contained a lot of nonsense. Was that true? Or was there something in it that you're worrying about? Or is it something else that's bothering you?'

Marian met his anxious look and held his gaze for a moment, before lowering her eyes again. He cared about her, she knew that. And she knew he wouldn't judge her. No matter what she told him.

'Archer? Do you ... do you have a couple of minutes?'

'Of course I do. And not just a couple of minutes, Marian. I can stay for as long as you want.'

If only that were true. She quickly dismissed that train of thought.

'Are you sure? This ... this might take a while.'

If she was going to tell him what was wrong, she needed to tell him everything.

Well, maybe not quite everything.

'I'm sure. Just let me send Elodie a text to let her know I'll be some time.'

'Thanks, Archer. I'll make us coffee while you do that.'

'What about your guests?'

'My guests? Oh. They'll be fine.'

For just a second there, she had almost forgotten about her guests.

All of them apart from one, that is.

Chapter 20

Marian was not sure where to start. Neither was she sure how much she wanted to tell him. Archer might be a close friend and someone she would trust almost completely, but the dynamic between them had changed, especially since Christmas.

It was not simply because she had realised that she loved him, and not just because he had fallen madly in love with Elodie.

It had changed because Marian had discovered that Stanley Talbot knew her secrets. Secrets she had thought no one knew but her.

It had changed because Archer now knew the whereabouts of his long-lost daughter. A daughter that he hoped would soon be part of his life.

It had also changed because many years before, Archer had invested time and money in another friend's business; a business that had recently been sold, making Archer an extremely wealthy man. Marian was as good as broke.

Not that Archer would ever let a simple thing like money come between him and his friends, Marian knew that. But she didn't want his pity and she didn't want him offering to lend her money to bail her out of the circumstances in which she now found herself. A situation she knew she should've dealt with sooner but had been too scared to face.

More importantly, it had changed because, instead of seeing one another every day, however briefly, as they had done for many, many years, Archer didn't come to the café as often these days, and Marian couldn't afford to spend much time at his pub.

Since Christmas they had drifted apart and in less than a couple of months it had felt, to Marian at least, that she and Archer were becoming strangers.

It was ridiculous and she knew it. She and Archer would always be good friends. But for her, the last two months had been difficult, to say the least. And the one person she might have been able to summon up the courage to turn to, had been so wrapped up with his new girlfriend and the exciting future that lay ahead of him, that he had not had either time, nor the inclination, to enquire as to how things were going in Marian's world. Until today.

And she did not blame him for that at all. Archer had had his own struggles, and he deserved every moment of the happiness he was now enjoying.

'I'm not sure where to start,' she said, twisting her mug of coffee around in circles on the table in the window where they sat. 'I've got so much on my mind, I'm spinning like a top.'

'I would say start at the beginning, but sometimes that's not the best place to start. Why don't you tell me what's on your mind today, and last night, and we'll see where we go from there?'

'That sounds so simple.'

'Things often are. We just don't see that at the time. When something is worrying us, or giving us pause for thought, we sometimes blow it out of all proportion. We spend all our time worrying about hundreds of possible outcomes, when what we really should be doing is dealing with the thing that caused the worry in the first place. What was it your mum used to say?'

'Everything happens for a reason.'

Archer smiled. 'Yes. But that wasn't the one I was thinking of.'

'Ask the Universe, and it will provide.'

He shook his head. 'It usually does. But no. Not that.'

'We could be here all day. Mum had a lot of sayings.' Marian sighed. 'I wish she were here right now. I miss her so much, Archer. Even after all these years. I miss them both.'

Archer reached out and squeezed the hand she had lain flat on the table.

'I know. They were wonderful people.' He smiled tenderly. 'I've remembered the saying I was thinking of. Although I may not have got it quite right. It was something along the lines of, "Just because we see one cloud in the sky, it doesn't mean there's a storm coming. But if you spend all day looking for clouds, then clouds are all you'll see. Instead, you should be looking for the sun."'

Marian raised her brows. 'Have you looked outside?' As if on cue, thunder rumbled in the distance. She smiled at Archer. 'I know what you're saying. Believe me, I've tried to look for solutions. Tried to look on the positive side. But I'm honestly not sure there is one. Not a pleasant one, anyway. Right.' She took a deep breath. 'Stanley knew things about me that I didn't think anyone knew. One of those things is that this café isn't doing as well as it once did. In fact, things are getting pretty desperate.'

'Since when? I have noticed it's been quiet in here on several occasions when I've popped in, but I thought that was simply down to my timing. Are you saying it's never busy anymore?'

Marian nodded. 'I think the last time Cove Café was full was about three years ago. Since then, it's become less and less busy every month. Even the last two summers weren't as good as I needed them to be. And we've had so much bad weather, especially this winter. People don't want to come all the way down here for a cup of coffee and a cake. They can get those in the Millside shopping centre, where not only can they stay warm and dry, they can have a choice of cafés. It's different for you. The Bow and Quiver is the only pub for a couple of miles. And everyone loves Bentley's food.'

'Then what we need to do is find a way to attract more customers to your café.'

'I've tried that, Archer. I've held coffee mornings for knitting clubs. Afternoon teas for the local Garden Society. Special lunch menus for old-age pensioners. You name it. Been there, done that. They all work for a while. But then the wind and rain arrive, even in the middle of summer, and suddenly Cove Café doesn't seem quite as appealing. By the time winter comes, I think many people have forgotten this café's even here.'

'Are things really as bad as they sound?'

'They're worse.'

'How much worse?'

'Not that bad, if you like all your bills in red. Dire, if you don't.'

'Okay. That's not a major problem. I've got money. We can get everything back in the black.'

Marian shook her head. 'No. Thank you for the offer, Archer. But no. If things carry on the way they are, and I can't see anything that could change them, I wouldn't be able to repay you.'

He squeezed her hand again. 'You don't have to repay me, Marian. We're friends.'

'I knew that's what you'd say. That's why I haven't told you before now.'

'Don't get angry. I'm trying to help.'

'By giving me money?'

'Yes. What's wrong with that?'

'Everything! Even if I paid all these bills, I'd still need money to keep the business going.'

'I'll give you money to do that.'

'No, Archer! You've got your own life to think about. You've got Elodie. You've got your daughter. You've got your business. You can't keep bailing me out. You can only plug so many holes in a sinking ship. I've used up all my savings. Every single penny. I need to earn a living. I need to get a job. I need ... I need to face reality and accept that I may have to ... sell this place.'

Marian burst into tears.

Archer was by her side in a second and he pulled her into his arms.

'No, Marian. Never. This is your home. You can't give this up.'

'I ... I ... may not ... have a ... choice,' she sobbed. 'I ... took out ... a loan two years ago ... and then another one after that. And then another one ... last year. I would try to get ... a mortgage, but I'd need to show ... an income to do that.'

'What? I had no idea things were so bad. Why didn't you tell me?'

'I ... was embarrassed. I ... I hoped to keep it a secret ... and pay it all back. But ... Stanley knew. He ... he knew, Archer! How did he know?'

Archer eased Marian from him and held her gently by the arms.

'Stanley knew a lot of things, Marian. How he knew them, we'll never find out. But he's dead and gone. We can pay your bills and clear the loans. We can clear all your debts. And then we'll devise a plan to get Cove Café back on its feet. Okay? And I won't hear no, so forget it. If you won't accept my money as a gift then we'll call it an investment. I'll invest in your business as a sleeping partner. No one else need know. What do you say to that?'

Marian blinked several times. 'You ... you don't know how much I owe.'

'I'm guessing it's not in the millions, so we should be fine. A few thousand? More than five but less than ten, I'm guessing.'

Marian gasped. 'How did you know that? Have you seen my file?'

He smiled affectionately. 'No. And I wouldn't have read it if I had seen it. I run a business too, Marian. I can estimate within reason, what your overheads here are likely to be. And don't forget I've known you all your life. Borrowing money is not something you would do lightly, so I can't imagine you would want to borrow very much. Why don't we get together tomorrow and add everything up? That'll give you time to get all your papers together. Okay?'

Marian nodded. 'And it'll give you time to think about it too. I'll completely understand if you change your mind. I can't ... I can't quite believe this is happening. But I don't want you to feel you have to do this, Archer. I don't expect anything from you.'

'I won't change my mind. I'm doing it because I want to, not because I feel I have to, Marian. How many times do I have to say this? We're friends. I'm lucky enough to have come into some money. If our roles were reversed, you'd do the same for me. Okay? That's one problem solved. What else is on your mind?'

Without thinking, Marian threw her arms around Archer's neck.

'Oh, Archer! I love you!'

'I love you too, Marian. Surely, after all these years, you must know that.'

Chapter 21

For a second – just one second, Marian thought all her dreams had come true.

She had not wanted to borrow money from Archer, but he had insisted. And then he had suggested becoming a sleeping partner in her business. That was even better.

Before Archer had taken over the pub from his parents, The Bow and Quiver had been an average hostelry. Nothing to write home about – just a place where the locals went for a pint, a packet of crisps, and a game of darts.

With Archer at the helm, or perhaps, behind the bar was more appropriate, the pub had become the place to be. People even travelled from other villages to frequent the newly updated establishment.

And when he opened the pub restaurant and employed Bentley as his chef, even

179

Archer admitted the 'fancy schmancy' meals, as some of the villagers referred to Bentley's food, became the main attraction.

Archer's profits had gone through the roof. Perhaps he could do something similar with Cove Café. Whether he did, or didn't, just the thought of having someone to share what had turned into a burden, made Marian feel more hopeful than she had been for some considerable time.

And then, when she had blurted out that she loved him, he had told her he loved her too.

She soon realised, of course, that Archer meant he loved her as a friend. And as she eased herself away, and looked into his eyes; eyes that were filled with sincere but platonic friendship, she thought perhaps the love she felt for him, however deep, however strong, was purely friendship too.

Perhaps the fear of losing that friendship had made her build it into something else. Or perhaps she was also just a little bit in love with him in a non-platonic way. It didn't really matter. He was head over heels in love with Elodie and that would never change. She knew him well enough to know that when Archer fell in love, he fell in love for keeps.

And now she also knew that she would never lose his friendship. It might need to adapt to take into account the changes all around them, but he had proved to her today, that whatever she needed, and whenever she needed it, she could count on him.

After that, she had even gone as far as telling him how much she thought she might be attracted to Parker, and about the kiss they had shared in the kitchen.

'It can't lead anywhere, I realise that. They'll be gone as soon as the weather clears.'

Archer beamed at her. 'But only for the season. He could come back later in the year. And he's here now, Marian, isn't he? Isn't life for living?'

She returned his joyful smile. 'That's what Mum would say.'

'Your mum was a smart woman. So I've only got one question. Why are you here with me when you could be upstairs with him? Unless you need to talk to me about anything else important, I suggest you go upstairs and I return to my pub.'

'You're the best, Archer Rhodes.'

Archer winked at her and headed towards the door, turning just before he opened it. 'Why don't you bring all four of your guests to the pub for a meal this evening? My treat. Unless of course, the storm is too severe. But if you can make it safely from here to there tonight, I'd really like to meet Parker and his friends.'

'That would be fabulous. Thank you so much, Archer.'

'I'll hopefully see you tonight.'

Marian waited until Archer had closed the door behind him and was halfway down the street before jumping up and down and spinning round and round. She hadn't felt this happy in years.

Oh wait. She had. She had felt like this when Parker kissed her.

She checked the sign on the door still said Closed, and ran upstairs as fast as she could. All four of them were in her sitting room. Nikki was fast asleep on the sofa, her head lolling back against the cushion. Bel sat beside her, flicking through a magazine that Iris had passed on to Marian. Magazines were a luxury Marian could not afford. Jasper was sitting sideways on one of the armchairs, his long muscular legs dangling over the arm. And Parker, who gave Marian a withering look when she rushed in to join them, was sitting on the window seat, staring out towards the bay whilst also scrolling on his phone.

'That was my friend, Archer Rhodes. I told you he owns the local pub. He's invited us all to his restaurant for a meal this evening, assuming the weather's not bad enough to prohibit us from going out.'

Bel glanced up from her magazine. 'Is that where you said the cordon bleu chef works? I can't remember his name.'

'Yes. And it's Bentley.'

'Great. I'm in. And so is Nikki. I can speak for her.'

'If Bel's in, so am I,' said Jasper.

'Fine.' Parker didn't look thrilled. 'We've got to eat.'

'Oh.' Marian had expected a little more enthusiasm than she received. 'Is 7 p.m. good for you all?'

Parker shrugged, Bel nodded, Jasper grinned and Nikki snored.

'I'll take that as a yes. Is anyone hungry? I'll go make some lunch.'

Bel tossed the magazine to one side. 'I'll help.'

'There's no need. I was only planning on having soup as we're going out for dinner tonight.'

'Home-made?'

'Er. From a can.'

'No.' Bel got to her feet. 'You've got plenty of vegetables, Marian. It'll only take twenty minutes.'

'It only takes three minutes from a can.'

Bel tutted. 'You say the funniest things. Next, you'll be telling us you cook pre-baked jacket potatoes in a microwave.'

'I do.'

Marian had a feeling Bel had already seen the bag of microwaveable jacket potatoes in her freezer.

'I can peel the veg,' Jasper said, throwing his legs to the floor and hurrying after Bel.

'Is *The Dream* still safe and sound?' Marian asked Parker, nodding towards the window where he sat.

'My dream? Or the yacht?'

'Er. Both?'

'So far, yes. And speaking of dreams, I see yours may have just come true.'

'Mine?'

Had he heard her conversation with Archer? And if so, how much of it?

'Uh huh. Didn't you tell me yesterday that you were in love with a friend? Bel tells me that friend is Archer. The one you rushed downstairs to see.' He got up from the seat and shoved his phone in his back pocket, walking towards the door as he did so. 'And you definitely looked … and sounded … *friendly.* I'm going for a walk. Tell Bel I'll be back in twenty minutes, please.'

By the time Marian realised what must have happened – that Parker had seen her and Archer hugging and probably telling one another that they loved each other – Parker was already gone.

Chapter 22

'That's odd,' Bel said. 'Parker's just texted to say he won't be back for lunch. He also says Iris is showing him around Millside.' She frowned at Marian. 'Who's Iris? And what's Millside?'

'Iris!' That came out as a cross between disbelief and annoyance. Marian hoped the others didn't notice. 'She's a friend. She was in the café yesterday when you arrived.'

'The one who flirted with Parker?' Bel looked even less pleased than Marian.

'Yes. Millside is the shopping centre on the outskirts of the village. I have no idea why Iris would want to show him that. Although she does love shopping.'

'Who doesn't?'

'Parker doesn't,' Nikki said.

'That's true.' Jasper looked confused. 'So why would he go shopping with some woman he doesn't even know. Was she hot? I can't remember.'

'She's gorgeous.' Marian's new-found happiness was slipping farther and farther away. 'She's a voice coach and she's just moved down from London. She still goes back regularly though, partly because she loves the city, and partly because she has several blue chip companies and private individuals, like actors, politicians, and such as clients. She's been seeing Bentley, the chef at The Bow and Quiver on and off, but it's nothing serious.'

'She doesn't sound like Parker's type,' Nikki said. 'And after Isabella, I can't see him being interested in a woman who's already seeing someone else.'

'Not for a relationship,' Bel said. 'Casual sex though, maybe. Sorry, Marian.'

'Don't be. I told you, nothing happened between us. It doesn't bother me if they have sex.' Perhaps if she told herself that enough times she would believe it.

'Apart from that kiss,' Jasper needlessly reminded her.

'You did say you liked him,' Nikki added. 'And I thought he liked you.'

'I think he does.' Bel texted a reply, and laid her phone face down on the worktop. 'But there seems to have been a bit of miscommunication. I said I thought things had moved on and that he'd probably got it wrong, but Parker didn't want to listen.'

Marian wondered what Bel's text had said. 'Miscommunication?'

Bel raised her brows. 'Apparently, Parker heard you and your friend, Archer telling one another how you felt, just now.'

'And he and I both saw you hugging,' Nikki said. 'Parker told me to pretend we hadn't. He thought it might make you feel awkward or something.'

It was just as Marian had suspected. And that obviously was not good.

'So you're saying Parker thinks I'm in love with Archer, and Archer's in love with me. Despite the fact that Archer's got a girlfriend he's crazy about. I can see how it might've looked but Archer and I are just good friends.'

'Greg and Parker were good friends,' Jasper said. 'But it didn't stop Greg and Parker's girlfriend, Isabella from cheating behind Parker's back. Friendships can lead to sex.' He winked at Bel. 'Really, really good sex. If given a chance.'

'You're getting on my last nerve, Jasper.' Bel glowered at him. 'I'm not sure I can take much more of this. How many more times do I have to say this? It is *never* going to happen. Ever. Not in this lifetime. Or the next.'

'When's he coming back?' Nikki asked. 'Did he say?'

Bel sighed loudly, picked up her phone, scrolled to the message, and shook her head.

'Nope. Just that he'll see us later. And if he's not back by 7.00, we should go to the pub without him.'

'Without him?' Marian had not expected that.

For some strange reason that hurt Marian as much as the thought of him and Iris having sex. She wanted to run to her bedroom, throw herself on the bed, and cry. She might have done exactly that, had she not received a text herself.

'Who's that?' Bel asked. Not that it was any of her business.

'It's Archer.' Marian was surprised. He had only left her about fifteen minutes earlier. 'Oh. He's got some news for me.'

'And?' Bel prompted.

'And he wants me to go to the pub this afternoon, if I'm free.'

She hoped he had not changed his mind already. Or that he had mentioned it to Elodie and she had told him to reconsider. But if the news was bad, he would not have sent her a text asking her to go to see him. He would have called, or more likely, returned to the café and broken the news face to face.

Marian wouldn't usually discuss her texts with people she hardly knew, but Bel, Nikki and Jasper already felt like friends. Parker did too, but maybe not so much now.

'He's dumped his girlfriend for you,' Jasper said. Not looking as if that was an entirely pleasing prospect.

Marian snorted derisively. 'I can assure you he hasn't. This is ... this is probably about the café. That's what we were discussing. I ... er. He might become a sleeping partner.'

'You're having sex with him?' Nikki shook her head. 'That was a joke. At least, I assume it was. You mean a sleeping partner in your business, don't you?'

'Yes. Business. Not sex.'

'Are you sure?' Jasper didn't look convinced.

'One hundred and ten per cent certain.'

'Do you want a sleeping partner in your business?' Bel queried. 'Don't take offence, but it seems pretty sleepy as it is.'

'And that's the point. Parker might be able to get the café buzzing again.' She laughed nervously. 'I'm not sure why I'm telling you all this.'

Why *was* she telling them all about her business? Or what she and Archer had discussed. It was as if, having opened up to Archer and told him just how bad the

189

situation was, she didn't need to keep it all a secret anymore.

That was pretty worrying. Especially as it wasn't her only secret.

But maybe keeping secrets wasn't such a good idea.

Besides, Stanley Talbot had known them all.

And as her mum had often said, 'Secrets have a way of coming out, no matter how hard we try to keep them hidden.'

Chapter 23

The wind was picking up once more as Marian made her way to Archer's pub. Thunder rumbled in the distance and lightning flashed on the horizon, but so far the torrential rain that had been forecast once again, held off. All morning there had been intermittent downpours and strong to gusting winds; either the tail end of yesterday's storm or the comparative lull before the storm that was yet to come but now the sky looked ominous and the air felt oddly oppressive. More like a tropical, summer storm than a wintry February freeze.

Marian pushed open the door of The Bow and Quiver and a blanket of heat hit her in the face. The place offered its usual warm welcome. Log fires crackled in the hearths and cheerful laughter mingled with animated conversations greeted her as she made her way to the bar.

'Is Archer around?' she asked.

'He's upstairs. He said to tell you to go straight up when you arrived.'

Marian walked around the side of the bar and to the stairs that led to Archer's home.

'It's me!' she called out, just to let him, and possibly Elodie, know that she was on her way.

'Come in,' Archer replied. 'I've opened a bottle of wine. It's lunchtime, after all. Have you eaten?' He reached out and took her coat, hanging it on a hook near the door.

Marian nodded and met his welcoming smile. 'Bel and I made soup. Home-made. Not from a can.'

'Isn't your soup always home-made?'

'When I serve it in the café, yes. When I make it for myself, not so much. It all seems such an effort when you're only cooking for one. I know I probably shouldn't be saying that. Especially if you're considering becoming a sleeping partner in my business. Are you still considering that? Or have you realised it's a lost cause, and changed your mind?'

'It's not a lost cause and I haven't changed my mind. Quite the opposite, in fact. Please come and sit down.'

Marian followed him to the sofa in front of the fire. The coffee table in between, had reams of documents and papers sprawled across the top. She sat down beside him and gratefully took the glass of wine he offered.

'Cheers!' He clinked his glass with hers.

'Cheers,' she repeated. 'Where's Elodie?'

He grinned. 'Catching up with sleep. As I said in the café, she was awake for most of the night.'

'Oh. I'm sorry I missed her. But I'll probably see her tonight.'

'She was asleep before I texted you. She doesn't know you're here.' He laughed suddenly. 'That sort of sounded a bit creepy. It's not, I promise you. But you know that.'

'It's a good thing I trust you,' Marian teased. 'You said you have news.'

'I do.' He took a sip of wine and then placed his glass on the table, moving some of the papers to make room. 'Shove them out of the way if you want to put your glass down.' He twisted on the seat to face her, and rested one arm on the back of the sofa. 'You know that El and I are planning a trip to see my daughter in the summer.'

Marian nodded but didn't speak.

'I've been trying to decide what to do about the pub while we're away. We'll be gone for at least a month. Maybe two. I've been considering a couple of options, one of which was leaving Bentley in charge. Another was employing a manager to run the place. But my preference was for Mum and Dad to come back and take it over for however long we're in Melbourne. We're not just planning to see my daughter, we're also visiting El's sister and brother-in-law. It would be good to know that we could stay for longer if we want to. Anyway, as I was walking back from your café, Mum called to confirm she and Dad are happy to come and hold the fort. So that solves that problem. And it opens up an opportunity. Which is what I wanted to talk to you about.'

'You're not going to offer me a job in your pub, are you?'

He looked surprised. 'That wasn't my intention, no. But if you want to do some part-time hours, I could certainly arrange that for you.' He laughed. 'You don't, do you?'

'Not particularly. Although I do need to earn some money and it's a very kind offer.'

He waved a hand in the air dismissively.

'Let's forget about that. I may have a better idea. You haven't been here for a meal for ages. In the pub restaurant, I mean. But you'll see when you come tonight, how packed it gets. We're having to turn people away. Especially at weekends.'

'I wish I had that problem in the café.'

'Yeah. And I'm certainly not complaining. Bentley's been nagging me for months to see if I can find a way to make room for more tables in the restaurant, but without some major structural work, there really is no way. So I've had an idea. An idea that I've briefly mentioned to Bentley and he's up for it, potentially. I didn't say how, or why, or when, but I said I thought there might be a chance of us being able to either use somewhere local as an overflow venue. Or to run it as a separate entity, but still under the pub's umbrella. I didn't mention Cove Café because I wanted to run it by you before I said anything more to anyone else. But it would make a lot of sense. It could be a café by day, and a restaurant by night, or just at weekends. I'm sure we could get the planners to agree. But it's just an idea at this stage. So what do you think? Obviously you'd need time to consider it properly. And numbers. We'd need to know that it would definitely make a profit. A profit that the three of us could share. We'd also pay you rent for the space. And you'd still have your home. Although I accept, having a restaurant below you might not be what you want.'

'Wow!'

'Please say no right now if you hate the idea. Don't feel in any way obligated. This is a completely separate notion. Our earlier

195

plan is still ready to go and I will have the money in your account tomorrow, in any event. No strings attached.'

Marian shook her head. 'No. I mean yes. I think it's a fantastic idea. And having a restaurant beneath me sounds like heaven. No more canned soup for me. I assume I'll get free food.' She laughed. 'I'm joking about the free food.'

'Free food every night will be part of the agreement.' He laughed too, and then he became serious. 'Do you really like the idea, Marian? I would hate you to say yes because you think you should, or something silly like that. I honestly don't mind at all if you say no. I can apply to build a conservatory at the back of the pub, or an extension, and we can fit more tables in that way.'

'I love the idea, Archer. But what will Elodie think?'

'I'm sure she'll love it too. But even if she doesn't, she wouldn't try to stop me going ahead with it. We both know that.'

'And Bentley? He would be happy that it was Cove Café?'

'I'm positive he will. Take some time to think about it. I'll get some figures together. And then you, me and Bentley can sit down and talk it through.'

'I don't know what to say, Archer. Apart from … thanks a million for being my friend. The best friend anyone could ever have.'

'I'm hardly that. I should've noticed you were struggling. I'm really sorry I didn't. But the future's looking bright. I think I can guarantee that. For all of us.'

Chapter 24

Marian had been unsure whether Parker would be joining them for dinner at the pub that night or not. Especially if things had gone well with him and Iris. Nevertheless, she had made an extra effort to look her best. The admiring look he had given her when she had walked into the sitting room that evening told her that she had done a good job.

'You're back!' She was overjoyed to see him.

'I'm back.'

His eyes swept over her like a caress, sending first a jolt of excitement when she had seen him standing by the window, and then a wave of tingling sensations throughout the length of her body.

'Did you like Millside?'

'Shopping centres aren't really my thing. I was impressed by the lake. No one was sailing today due to the weather but it looks as though it's a great place to learn. I like the fact that part of it's an ice rink in the winter and a rollerblade or skate park in the summer. The developers worked hard to make it look as natural and yet as aesthetically pleasing as possible.'

'They did. Did you ... stay there long?'

Parker shook his head slowly, his gaze fixed firmly on her face.

'Not that long. Iris wanted to show me Clementine Cottage.'

'I bet she did,' Marian mumbled.

'Sorry? I didn't quite catch that.' His brows moved closer together. 'It's a very pretty cottage, and it has sensational views. You can almost see the entirety of Clementine Cove – the village and the bay.'

'I know. It's beautiful.'

'With the telescope, I was able to see every detail of *The Dream*. Also of your café. And the pub.'

'That must've been ... thrilling.'

Marian could feel a frisson of excitement building, despite the inconsequential topic of conversation.

'It was ... interesting. Did you enjoy your afternoon?'

'Very much so, thank you. My good friend, Archer made me an offer that could completely change my life.'

Something flashed across his eyes.

'What sort of offer? Or is that none of my business?'

'It's a business proposal. You weren't here when I was telling the others what Archer and I had been discussing in the café earlier today.' She took a few steps towards him. 'And I think there might have been some sort of ... misunderstanding, on your part.'

'Misunderstanding?'

'Yes.' She hurried on without really thinking; she needed to make him understand. 'The fact is, the café isn't doing as well as it once did. I'm struggling, financially. Archer offered to help me out. Like the wonderful friend he is. And I love him for doing that. And the reason he is doing it, is because we've known each other all our lives and he loves me. As a friend. Just as a friend. Nothing more. And I feel the same way about him. I thought it might be something deeper. But it isn't. I realise that now.'

'I see. Thank you for telling me. That's good to know.'

'Iris is lovely, isn't she?'

'Oh for God's sake, you two!' Bel's words of irritation startled both Marian and Parker. Neither had seen her standing in the doorway, but clearly she had been there for a little while. 'She's telling you she's not in love with Archer. She's not, Parker. And she wants to know if you had sex with Iris. He didn't, Marian. Now will you two just bloody well kiss one another. The three of us are starving and we want to go to dinner.'

Marian gasped in surprise. And as she turned to look at Bel, only then did she see Nikki and Jasper also hovering in the doorway.

'We'll be downstairs,' Bel continued. 'You've got two minutes. No time for anything other than a kiss.' A huge grin swept across her face. 'Sex will have to wait till later,' she added, ushering Nikki and Jasper towards the stairs.

Chapter 25

Dinner at The Bow and Quiver was as delicious as Marian knew it would be. The restaurant was packed, as Archer had told her to expect. But Marian had better things than a wonderful meal in perfect company, on her mind.

To her surprise, the moment Bel had left them earlier, Parker had marched over to her, taken her by the arms, looked into her eyes for just a moment with that crooked smile dancing on his lips, and without a word, he had kissed her.

She had kissed him back with equal enthusiasm and that second kiss she and Parker had shared was even better than the first. Neither of them had wanted it to end. But Bel had yelled up the stairs, threatening to come up and drag them out by their ears. They had burst out laughing and reluctantly agreed they had to go.

'We'll pick this up later, if that's okay with you?' he had asked, teasing his fingers through her hair and brushing her lips with his one last time.

'Uh-huh,' was all she could manage to say.

He had held her hand a few minutes later, as they, together with Nikki, Bel and Jasper had struggled through the increasingly strong winds to reach the pub. As they all stepped inside, the heavens opened and torrential rain pummelled the roof of The Bow and Quiver and splashed into the ever deepening puddles in the road outside.

Archer and Parker hit it off the moment they met. As had Bel and Bentley. But on a totally different level.

Archer had often sailed in his youth and he, Parker and Jasper chatted about boats; the engines, their speed in knots, the sleek line of the keel, the broadness of the beam, the overall construction. GPS, chart plotters, radar, autopilot, satellite communication – they all seemed fascinating to the men.

Marian considered making a crude remark when seacocks were mentioned, but instead she, Elodie, Bel and Nikki discussed the more important and more interesting – to them – items on a yacht, such as the kitchen and its equipment.

'*The Dream* has a country kitchen configuration,' Bel said. 'There's a surprisingly large, open, stainless steel galley, and a dinette for use of the crew, almost as spacious. There's also a separate, formal dining area for our clients. There are five state rooms, accommodating ten guests. There's also a master suite with a private deck on the wheelhouse deck. That's Parker's but he'll be renting it out and bunking with the rest of us crew most of the time. We have four crew bunks.'

'Bunks as opposed to cabins?' Elodie asked.

Elodie had never been on board a yacht but Marian had. Not a superyacht like *The Dream*, though. Like Archer, Marian had sailed when she was younger but it wasn't something she had time for very much these days. She had enjoyed it, but it was never a passion as it clearly was for Parker and Jasper, and also for Bel and Nikki.

'They're still called cabins on a superyacht,' Nikki said. 'But they're tiny and fairly basic compared to the guest cabins, although each one does have a small en-suite. We've got two bunks to each crew cabin, which are at the stern. That's the back of the yacht. The guest cabins are located towards the bow. That's the front.'

'There's a large aft deck,' Bel continued. 'With a hot tub and plenty of outdoor seating, together with an al fresco dining area. The forward deck has a lounge and sunbathing area with the comfiest sun beds, and then up a flight of stairs from that there's a large flybridge. There's a bar, sun loungers, and a huge L-shaped sofa along with coffee tables. Down on the swim platform, there're hot and cold showers and a few 'toys' stashed away. Like an inflatable slide, paddleboards, lilos, snorkelling equipment and a couple of jet skis.'

'Wow!' Elodie exclaimed. 'That sounds expensive. How much did the yacht cost? Do you know?'

Bel glanced at Parker and shrugged. 'Just under one point five million, I think. But it needed some work. Parker spent two years and a lot more cash doing it up to get it the way he wanted.'

Marian nearly choked on her drink. 'One and a half million *pounds*?'

Bel nodded. 'Yachts aren't cheap. Especially yachts like *The Dream*. She's thirty-four metres long so she's a superyacht. Superyachts are usually anything more than twenty-four metres up to around fifty. Anything over fifty is a mega yacht, and there's no limit to how long they can go. I think the largest is around one hundred and eighty-three metres. And we're talking billions, not millions for those. But there's one being built, so Jasper says, that will be around the two-hundred and twenty-two metre mark. It's due to launch in another two years' time and that'll be even more eye-wateringly expensive.'

'I can't believe there are people with that much money.' Marian said. 'And this is just for a boat. Imagine how much their homes must cost.'

Bel grinned. 'People who can afford mega yachts usually have several homes all over the world. And money isn't a problem. They don't need to worry about how much things cost.'

'I wish I could say the same,' Marian said.

'Where are you going to be based?' Elodie asked. 'Or should I say moored?'

'Based is fine,' Nikki said. 'And we'll be based in Antibes. Parker's dad has a friend who owns a luxury hotel there. That's where a lot of our clients will be staying before or after they come aboard *The Dream*.'

'We're lucky to have that contact,' Bel said, 'As newcomers, it can be hard to find the right clients, but we're already booked up for much of the season. And we've got several more clients via Parker and his dad's other business. Which is a luxury car dealership.'

'Parker's a car salesman,' Bel said, smiling affectionately despite the slightly demeaning tone. 'That doesn't sound quite as sexy as the captain of a luxury yacht, somehow, does it?'

'Oh, I don't know.' Marian defended him. 'I think luxury cars are very sexy. And so are the people who sell them.'

Elodie smiled. 'Parker certainly is. If I weren't so madly in love with Archer, you'd have competition, Marian. In fact, you already have. Iris was going on and on about him just this afternoon.'

'Oh? What was she saying?' Marian glanced at Parker but he, Archer and Jasper were still deep in conversation.

'Just that they'd bumped into one another outside your café and she offered to show him the lake at Millside. And then she took him back to Clementine Cottage and showed him around. She said she flirted relentlessly but the guy didn't seem at all interested and she wondered if he was gay.'

Nikki spat her drink across the table in surprise. 'God! I almost choked.' She laughed. 'Does your friend think that just because a guy isn't interested in her, he must be gay?'

Elodie frowned. 'No. But most men are interested in her. Or they have been in all the years I've known her. She only likes men who are blond, and preferably blue-eyed, so she's very picky.'

'Well, Parker's not gay,' Bel said. 'But he is very picky too. And he didn't pick your friend, it seems. Talking of blond men, Bentley's gorgeous, isn't he?'

'And he's dating Iris,' Elodie said, although she was smiling. 'She should be here later. She had an urgent call from one of her clients who needed some tips for a presentation they've got to give in the morning.'

'If she's dating Bentley,' Bel asked, 'why was she flirting with Parker this afternoon?'

Elodie sighed. 'I don't know. She does it a lot and that's what I keep asking her.'

'It's almost a shame I'm going away,' Bel said.

Bentley came to the table where they sat. They had been introduced earlier and he'd asked Bel if she would like to join him in the kitchen later. She had, of course, said she'd love to, and he'd told her he'd come and get her once he'd finished a couple of things he needed to get done before he forgot.

'Hey, everyone. Hey, Bel. Want to come and join me?'

Bel shot to her feet. 'Absolutely. Lead the way. I'm right behind you.' She turned and gave Marian, Nikki and Elodie a huge thumbs up, a wink and an open-mouthed scream of excitement before following Bentley to the kitchen.

'How long are you all going to be away for?' Elodie asked.

'The season runs from May until September or October, depending on the weather,' Nikki said.

'Oh. Why are you leaving so early then?' Marian queried.

'Most yachts come from their winter ports, like the Caribbean, between February and May. We were originally planning to leave Northumberland in late March. But we left early thanks to Isabella and Greg's wedding.'

'Who're Isabella and Greg?' Elodie asked. 'Are they getting married in the Med?'

'No,' Nikki said. 'They got married on Monday in Broadlands Bay, in Northumberland.

'Isabella is Parker's ex-girlfriend,' Marian informed Elodie. 'He didn't want to stick around and watch the love of his life marry his best friend.'

'Former best friend,' Nikki corrected. 'And former love of his life, I think. Shall I get another round of drinks in? If we wait for the guys to get them, we'll all die of thirst.'

Chapter 26

'Bentley's an incredible chef,' Bel gushed, during one of her many returns to the table where the others were all seated for dinner. 'No wonder this place is packed.'

'He's not bad looking either,' Jasper grumbled. 'If you like that whole blond hair and blue-eyed thing.'

'I do,' Bel said. 'Sorry, Jasper.'

Jasper shrugged. 'That's fine. I can handle a bit of competition.'

'There is no competition,' Bel said. 'Believe me, Jasper. Please, for once in your life, *believe me.*'

'Whatever.' Jasper shrugged again.

'I hope you're not thinking of jumping ship,' Parker joked, a hint of concern evident in his tone.

'Nah. Besides, he's seeing Iris. Or so he thinks. Not that their relationship is likely to go anywhere. Bentley and I have exchanged contact details. He's promised to email me some of his recipes and we're going to keep in touch.'

Marian still had no idea what, if anything, had happened between Iris and Parker, but he had told Bel nothing had, and from what Elodie had said, Iris had complained about that very fact. So for now, that was good enough. Later, when she was alone with him, Marian could ask for details. She needed to know, for some reason, whether Parker was attracted to Iris, or not. She hoped she would like the answers that she got.

But she had to keep reminding herself that Parker would be leaving. Whatever this was, this thing that both of them were feeling, it could not go anywhere. As soon as the weather cleared, which was likely going to be in just a day or two, Parker and his friends would be sailing off towards the Med. Marian would be staying in her cottage and running Cove Café.

At least now she had a happier future to look forward to as far as her business was concerned. If Archer's latest ideas took off – and she had every reason to believe they would – she should even be able to pay him back for all the loans and debts of hers that he was clearing. And she would still be in profit after that, if they reached the projected figures he had emailed her that afternoon, a few hours after their meeting. Archer, it seemed, was even more excited about their future plans than she was.

She could not believe how much everything could change within a matter of days – of hours, regarding her business. Of two days, regarding her heart.

She didn't want to think about how she would feel when Parker sailed *The Dream* out of the bay. She knew he had to go. She knew she had to stay.

'Everything happens for a reason.'

She could hear her mum's words in the warmth and laughter and friendship surrounding her that evening.

But she couldn't quite work out what that reason was.

And later, as she and Parker dashed back to her cottage, hand in hand, trying and failing, to dodge the torrential rain whilst being almost knocked off balance by the battering winds, a tiny part of her wondered if *The Dream* might sustain some damage in this second storm and not be seaworthy enough to sail.

She didn't wish that would happen, of course. To wish for something bad to befall someone you cared about was mean and cruel and selfish. She would never do that to Parker.

But during dinner he had looked at her in a way that made her feel that she was the most beautiful woman in the world ... or at least in the pub. He'd also made her certain that they were going to have incredible sex that night. And she had a feeling it was going to be the best night of her life.

For one brief moment, memories, doubts and fears came thundering to the fore, but Parker had smiled at her and the memories had melted away.

'Don't let the past dictate your future,' her mum would no doubt say, if she were here today.

And she would be right. Living in the past does nothing other than stops you moving on and making the most of your present and your future. And with any luck, tonight, and definitely tomorrow, Marian would be able to enjoy both.

Without thinking, she had sent a silent plea out into the Universe.

'Please find a way to make Parker stay. Or for us to be together. Even if it's just for a while.'

Because as her mum had also often said, "Ask the Universe, and it will provide."

Chapter 27

Marian was expecting to have incredible sex with Parker, a man she hadn't been able to stop thinking about since almost the first time she had seen him. She wasn't expecting to find herself – and Parker – in the middle of a massive drama. Although 'drama' was hardly the appropriate word to use to describe what happened that night.

They were all soaking wet and freezing cold on returning from The Bow and Quiver, but everyone was laughing happily and making jokes.

They were full to bursting with delicious food; telling stories of some of the villagers they had met; and each one of them was more than a little tipsy from the copious amounts of wine, followed by the liqueurs they had consumed. Marian and Parker less so than the others, but even Marian felt mellow and relaxed in the way that only alcohol – and perhaps some illegal drugs, she wouldn't know about that – could make you feel.

As eager as Marian was to be alone with Parker, when Bel had suggested they all have some of the homemade lemon liqueur that Bentley had given her, Marian felt she couldn't say no. Bel had held the bottle aloft and waved it in the air from side to side.

'It tastes just like the real stuff,' Bel said.

'Don't you think that maybe you've had enough alcohol for one night?' Parker suggested.

'No,' Bel said, almost losing her balance. 'Who are you? My father?'

'I have,' Nikki said. 'I'm going to bed.'

'You can't!' Bel insisted. 'Just one more drink. Just one.'

Nikki had relented.

Parker looked Marian in the eye, grimaced as if it was the last thing he wanted to do, and then also shrugged in defeat.

'I suppose one more glass can't do any harm.'

He was soon regretting those words.

It had all seemed so innocent at first.

Marian got the glasses; Nikki poured the drink because Bel's hand was a little unsteady and Jasper reached out to stop Bel from falling over.

215

'Get off me, you ... you, ex-yeti.' Bel shoved his hand away with one of hers, and scowled at him.

He held both hands in the air in a gesture of surrender.

'Just trying to help. You're so drunk you can hardly stand up.'

'Drunk! I'm nowhere near drunk.'

Bel proceeded to knock back the glass of lemon liqueur Nikki had poured, and then reached for a second. In her haste and her drunken state, she knocked the bottle out of Nikki's hand and it smashed onto Marian's polished wood floor, spilling its contents over the rug in front of the fire.

'Oops,' she said, grinning. 'S-orry.'

'Okay, Bel.' Parker sounded angry. 'That's quite enough.'

'It's okay.' Marian was glad it was only the bottle that had broken and not the glasses that had belonged to her mum and dad. 'Accidents happen.'

'I'll clear it up,' said Nikki.

'I can do it.' Marian said.

Nikki smiled kindly. 'It's what I do, Marian. You wouldn't believe the amount of bottles, glasses and crockery that get broken during a yacht charter season.'

Jasper and Parker were already picking up pieces of glass.

'I think we need to get Bel to bed,' Parker said.

Bel had now collapsed onto the sofa and looked as if she had fallen asleep. Or possibly passed out.

'Is she okay?' Marian was a little concerned.

'Yeah.' Parker seemed accustomed to Bel's behaviour. 'She has done this a few times, recently. She assured me it won't happen when we're on charter, and I believed her. Perhaps I need to have another word with her about it. She's been going through a pretty tough time over the last few years.'

'Yes.' Marian nodded. 'We talked about it yesterday.'

'You did?' He seemed surprised. 'That's good. Perhaps that means she's coming to terms with it all.'

'I'll get her to bed.' Jasper placed the shards of glass on one of the magazines on the coffee table. 'Is it okay if I leave those there for now?'

'I'll get a dustpan and brush.' Marian turned towards the kitchen.

'I think a vacuum cleaner might be better,' Nikki suggested.

Jasper gently lifted Bel into his arms and, as if she weighed no more than a piece of glass, he carried her towards the bedroom in which she had spent the previous night.

Parker got the vacuum cleaner out of Marian's kitchen cupboard and Nikki switched it on. He then helped Marian take the glasses into the kitchen, and once there, he pulled her softly into his arms.

'Clearing up Bel's mess wasn't quite how I expected to be spending this part of the evening.'

'It'll only take a few more minutes,' Marian whispered. 'And then we'll have all night.'

'You are sure this is what you want, aren't you?'

'Absolutely certain.'

'I ... I'll still be leaving once the weather clears.'

'I know you will. So we had better make the most of the time we have.'

'I can come back, you know. When the season's over.'

Marian smiled up at him, pressing her body closer into his.

'There's nothing I would love more, Parker. But perhaps we shouldn't make promises we may not be able to keep.'

He was about to say more, but she planted her lips softly onto his and his arms tightened around her as he responded to her touch.

At first, Marian thought the sound she heard above the white noise of the vacuum cleaner, was the wind, and it took her a couple of seconds to disengage her mind and body from the passionate kiss with Parker.

The vacuum cleaner stopped, allowing the sound to become clearer.

'Was that a scream?'

She had hardly said the words before Parker was racing along the hall towards Bel's bedroom.

Bel was screaming, Jasper was shouting, and things were being thrown.

'He was ... he was ... I don't know what he was trying to do,' Bel shrieked.

'I was trying to take your dress off,' Jasper growled, holding one hand over a cut on his cheek. A cut that was probably caused by being hit with the vase that now lay broken on the carpet.

'You were going to ... rape me!' Bel yelled, in disbelief.

'Shit no!' Jasper was clearly horrified. As was everyone else. 'Of course, I wasn't. I would never do anything to hurt you. How could you even think that?'

'Then why were you undressing me!' She held the bedside lamp in her hand, poised to launch it at Jasper.

Marian dashed forward at the same time as Parker.

'Please don't throw that lamp,' Marian pleaded. It may have been a completely inappropriate time to worry about a lamp, but it was an anniversary present she had given to her parents. 'It means a lot to me.'

'More than me being sexually assaulted!'

'Of course not.' Marian wasn't sure what to do.

'I wasn't sexually assaulting you! Shit, Bel. Is that really what you think?'

'We know you weren't,' Parker said, stepping between Bel and Jasper. 'But we can all understand why Bel might think you were. Undressing her wasn't a good idea. Surely you must see that?'

'I didn't want her dress to get creased. She loves that dress.'

'Perhaps you should've woken her up and asked,' Nikki said.

'I didn't think I was doing anything wrong. I've seen her in her underwear loads of times.'

'That's the excuse all men make,' Bel hissed. 'You've been mauling me and harassing me for months. You're constantly touching me and you seem to think it's all okay. It isn't, Jasper. I should call the police and have you arrested.'

'For what? For trying to make you comfortable? For being a friend? If it had been Nikki undressing you, would you have been upset? Jesus, Bel. We've been friends for years. I would never try to take advantage of you. Never!'

'I think we should all sit down and talk about this,' Parker said, looking as if he had no idea what he was doing. 'You're understandably upset, Bel. And you're right. Jasper shouldn't have done what he did. And he shouldn't keep harassing you. But that's partly my fault. I should've said something. I should've told him it was inappropriate. I didn't realise how ... uncomfortable it was making you feel. Like him, I ... I thought it was all just friendly teasing.'

'Friendly teasing! Is that what you call it. I can't believe you, Parker. You told me yourself this afternoon that when that woman, Iris kept throwing herself at you today, it made you feel uncomfortable. I told you then, times that feeling by ten and you might understand how Jasper makes me feel.'

'Yes. But...' He shot a look at Marian, and then at Nikki before shaking his head and lowering it in what was clearly a gesture of shame. 'I'm sorry, Bel. I truly am. I should've done something to help you. But I honestly hadn't realised how bad it was making you feel.'

Jasper stared at her. 'Does it really upset you that much? I ... I had no idea. I promise you. That was never my intention. I ... I thought we were friends. I thought it was all a joke. I'm mortified, Bel. Genuinely mortified. I don't know what more I can say. Except, I'm really, truly sorry. And I can promise you it will never, ever happen again. If there's anything else I can do to make you feel okay, I'll do it. Just tell me. Do you … Do you want me to leave *The Dream*? I will, if that is what you need me to do.'

Everyone looked at Bel.

'You're safe, Bel,' Nikki said, walking towards her and taking the lamp from her clenched fingers. 'And you know, deep down, Jasper would never hurt you. They're not the only ones at fault. I thought it was all just teasing, too. I didn't realise it was genuinely upsetting you. We all misunderstood the situation. We all misread the signs. We all need to learn from this. But you know Jasper is your friend, and that he truly cares about you. I realise it's not the same. And believe me, I'm in no way trying to demean or dismiss what you've been going through. But sometimes, when you're really bitchy, that hurts me.'

Bel gasped, blinked several times, and finally stared at Nikki with her mouth half open.

'You don't do that on purpose,' Nikki continued. 'And I can see by the expression on your face you're surprised. But that's the thing, Bel. There are some genuinely dreadful people in the world. People who will behave like the creeps, or bullies, or thugs they are. And then there are those who hurt people they care about without realising they're doing it. Jasper is one of the good guys, Bel. You know that. And you also know that, due to all the crap you've had to go through over the last few years, you've changed. You can be really cruel sometimes, even though you don't mean to. Jasper is, and probably always will be, a little bit in love with you. But he's not a creep. He's not a bully. He's not a thug. And he's not a sexual predator. And now he knows he needs to change his behaviour towards you. Towards all women. He will. You know that.'

'I will,' Jasper promised. 'And I'll stay as far away from you as you need me to.'

'Oh, God,' Bel exclaimed. 'I don't know what I want. And my head is pounding so much I can't think straight. At least the shock has sobered me up. Nikki's right, I know. And I do like you, Jasper. As a friend. You've helped me a lot, over the years I've known you. I just wish … I just wish you would leave me alone. I used to like the way you would put your arms around me when I was upset. So I can understand why this is so confusing for you. It's confusing for me too. I don't know when your 'friendly hugs' became creepy for me. But they did. And that makes me sad. But it also makes me angry. If I ask you to back off, you should back off. If I ask you not to touch me, you shouldn't touch me. I don't want you to leave *The Dream* because of me. And I don't want to leave because of you. You frightened me tonight. I woke up to find you undressing me and I, perhaps, overreacted. If we can get past this, be respectful of one another, be friends and nothing more, that would make me happy. But things would have to change. Can you understand that?'

'Yes. I can. I know I can.'

Bel let out a long and sorrowful sigh. 'God. What a mess. What a complete and utter mess.' She shot a look at Marian. 'Oh hell, Marian. I've just realised I've broken some of your things.'

'Don't worry about that. The important thing is, you're okay. Everyone's okay. That's all that matters.'

'Shall I make some tea?' Nikki asked. 'I'm not sure any of us will get much sleep tonight.'

'I'd like a cup of tea,' Bel said. She looked at Jasper. 'And maybe we can talk?'

'I'd like that,' Jasper said. 'And I promise to sit on the other side of the room.'

'Was that meant to be a joke?' Nikki asked.

'No. I was being serious. Bel needs space.'

Nikki frowned. 'Not that much space. We'll be living on a boat, remember, once the weather clears.'

'No,' Bel said, a very small smile forming on her lips. 'I don't need that much space. Not now you seem to understand. Let's try sitting at opposite ends of the sofa and see how I feel about that.'

Jasper reached out to help her off the bed on which she had been standing but quickly withdrew his hand.

'Sorry. Old habits.'

'You're learning,' Parker said. 'That's what matters.'

'I've completely ruined your night,' Bel gasped, looking at Parker and Marian.

'You haven't,' Marian lied.

'There'll be other nights,' Parker said.

'It's only midnight,' said Nikki. 'I'll stay up with Bel and Jasper, if you two want to go to bed.'

'Er. I'm not entirely sure it's appropriate,' Parker said. 'Perhaps we should all sit up and talk.'

'Oh for God's sake, Parker,' said Bel. 'Let's not make this whole thing even worse. We'll be fine. I think.'

Chapter 28

Marian and Parker hesitated for a while.

Bel and Nikki headed for the kitchen, but Jasper offered to make the tea and told them to wait for him in the sitting room, obviously wanting to ensure he gave Bel her space. He picked up the pieces of the broken vase and left a few moments later.

'There's antiseptic in the bathroom cupboard, and some plasters,' Marian informed him as he went. 'You might want to wash and dress that cut.'

'Thanks,' he said, and smiled. 'But I think a cut's the least of my worries.'

'I'm here if you need me,' Parker said.

Jasper nodded. 'Yeah. I know.'

Parker turned to face Marian, stretching out his arms but stopping short of placing them around her waist.

'It makes you stop and think. I knew, when Bel told us to kiss today that you were happy about it, but yesterday, I didn't ask if I could put my arms around you, or kiss you last night. Should I have?'

Marian shook her head. 'No. I wanted you to.'

'But what if you hadn't? What if I had misread the situation?'

'You didn't. But it's difficult, I agree. Did you honestly feel uncomfortable with Iris throwing herself at you today?'

He nodded. 'Yes. But it was nothing compared to the way Bel has obviously been feeling.' He sighed. 'I really want to spend the night with you, Marian. But I have to be honest. What happened in here has sort of killed the mood. This is probably the last thing you would expect to hear from a guy, but could we just sit and talk? And maybe, cuddle.'

Marian smiled. 'That sounds nice. Come with me.'

She slid her hand in his and led him to her bedroom, closing the door behind them and turning on the bedside light.

He looked out into the darkness as the wind rattled the window frame, rain pelted the pane, and thunder crashed in the distance.

'I'd almost forgotten there was a storm,' he said.

'You wouldn't be here if there wasn't.'

He met her gaze as she sat down on her bed and pulled him towards her.

'No. I suppose I wouldn't. I know I shouldn't say this, but I'm glad this problem with Bel and Jasper came to a head here rather than on the yacht and at sea. I think it would've been worse somehow if we were all miles from land. *The Dream*'s fairly spacious but it's still a confined space.'

'Bel might've been tempted to throw Jasper overboard. But I know I shouldn't joke about it.'

'*I* might've been tempted to do the same.' Parker gave her a wry smile. He glanced down at their entwined fingers. 'I like Archer. And Elodie too. And Bentley. I had a really good time tonight. Until just now.'

'Me too.'

'You looked so beautiful. I couldn't keep my eyes off you.'

'Thanks.' Heat rushed to her cheeks. And to other parts of her body. 'Apart from when you, Archer and Jasper were talking about boats,' she teased.

He laughed at that, looked up from their hands, and gazed directly into her eyes.

She needed to control what she was feeling. He had said he wasn't in the mood for sex, and she had felt the same, but right now, with that gorgeous crooked smile tugging at his mouth, she wanted to throw him back against the pillows and strip him naked.

But maybe she should ask him first?

'I want you to see *The Dream*,' he said. 'Once the storm has blown itself out and fine weather's forecast, I'd like you to come on board and I'll show you around. Maybe we can take her out and you can see what she's capable of. Archer told me you and he sailed when you were younger. You didn't mention that.'

'You didn't ask. I don't know why I didn't tell you. I suppose it was because it was such a long time ago.'

'Did you enjoy it?'

''Very much. But not as much as you clearly do.'

He breathed deeply. 'With me, it's a passion. I get itchy feet if I haven't been out for more than two days in a row.'

'That means you must be starting to get itchy feet. Although you did go on board yesterday. Does that count?'

He grinned. 'Not really. Archer also told me you've lived here all your life. In this cottage.'

'Wow.' She laughed, but a little nervously. 'And there was I thinking you were talking about boats when, in fact, you were talking about me. What else did Archer tell you?'

He held her gaze. 'That he trusts you with his life. That you're kind and caring and thoughtful. That any man would be lucky to have you by his side.'

'Is that all?' She laughed again. 'Damn. I also paid him to tell you he thought I was the most beautiful woman in the world. And that once you've been to bed with me you will never want to leave. Oh! Not that he would know what I'm like in bed. We haven't slept together. Bugger. I shot myself in the foot there, didn't I?'

He laughed and then grew serious. 'I don't want to leave. And I haven't slept with you yet.'

His face closed in on hers and his kiss was soft and tender. But passion soon flared and the kiss quickly deepened. Their hands were on one another's bodies, exploring, touching, caressing. It didn't take long for their clothes to be tossed onto the floor.

Marian had expected Parker to be good in bed, although she had nothing on which to base that expectation. He exceeded everything she had imagined. And she had imagined rather a lot. She had tossed and turned in bed the previous night, imagining.

He surpassed each and every scenario. Each kiss, each touch, each caress, each thrust. Every move he made sent stronger sensations of pleasure shooting through her.

And after they finally climaxed, all she managed to say was, 'Oh, my God, Parker!'

And Parker said almost the same, but he moaned Marian's name.

Chapter 29

One minute Parker felt elated, the next, miserable.

The storm had raged all night and was still making its presence known as twilight crept in through a gap in the curtains, although the windows in Marian's bedroom were not rattling quite as much now and the bullets of rain hitting the panes seemed fewer. But it was not the weather that had kept him awake. It was the rollercoaster of his emotions.

After what Isabella and Greg had done, he had been determined to stay away from relationships. He had told himself that there was no way he was going to take a chance on love, and get his heart smashed to pieces again. At least, not for a long time.

And it had only been a little over three months since Isabella had dumped him and turned his world on its head. He thought it would take many months, possibly even years, to get over her and the pain she had inflicted on him.

Merely a few days ago, he had been foolish enough to venture out into the path of an oncoming storm, in his beloved yacht, just so that he did not have to hear the church bells of St Benedict's announcing that Isabella and Greg were now husband and wife.

He had risked not only his yacht and the future he had been planning for so many years, but also the lives of his crew; his best friends. And for what?

To sail into a safe harbour seeking shelter from the storm, and to fall crazily in love at first sight with another woman?

No way. It was ridiculous.

Yet he felt wonderful.

He wanted to shout her name from the rooftops. To hold her in his arms and never let her go. He wanted to kiss her every morning and every night ... and every hour of every day. He wanted to make love with her again and again and again.

He couldn't believe he could feel this happy. This hopeful. This fantastic.

But...

Assuming she felt the same – and he had every reason to believe she did – what then?

For this to develop into a relationship and for them to have a future together it meant he would have to give up his dream, so that he could stay with her. The dream he had had for almost his entire life. The dream he had worked so hard for. All those extra jobs he had done just to add a few more pounds to his growing nest egg, would have been for nothing.

But if he had not done those extra jobs, he would not have got to know Jack Thorpe. And without Jack's amazingly kind and exceedingly generous bequest, Parker would not have been able to afford to buy *The Dream*, two years ago. Or to have spent the last two years carrying out repairs and refurbishments to get her, not just shipshape, but sleek, elegant and breathtakingly beautiful. He might be biased, but for a superyacht of her size, she was absolutely stunning and at the top of her class. And even if he stayed in Clementine Cove to be with Marian, he would still have his beloved yacht. So at least he would have achieved part of his dream.

What other choice did he have?

Unless Marian gave up everything she had in Clementine Cove to be with him? Somehow, he could not see her doing that. Archer had told him last night that Marian had lived in the village her entire life. She had a business here. A business she loved. It might be a business that was currently struggling, but it seemed she and Archer had plans to turn things around on that front. If Marian was making plans to put her business on a firmer footing, she would definitely not consider leaving.

Archer had also said that Marian had inherited the cottage from her deceased parents whom she adored. She had been so determined to remain in the family home that she had found a way to earn a living from there. Another reason she would want to stay. The cottage was her link to her parents. Would she ever be willing to let it go?

But if he stayed, assuming Marian didn't cheat on him, or dump him for some other reason and their relationship grew, would he resent the fact that he had given up so much to be with her? Would being with Marian make up for all that he would lose?

And what about Bel, Nikki and Jasper? They had also planned their futures around him and his dream. They had given up other potential jobs to spend the entire summer season in the Med, aboard *The Dream*. And possibly the winter season in the Caribbean, or wherever Parker and the three of them decided they wanted to go. He couldn't let them down. He couldn't tell them they would have to make other arrangements. Find other jobs as crew on another yacht. He couldn't do that to them. They weren't just crew and they weren't merely employees, they were friends. Good friends.

Was it possible that he could continue to follow his dream and still have a relationship with Marian? He could delay his departure for a week or two but to have a successful season he would need to be in the Med by mid-to-late March. And he would not be back until September or October. Could they keep their relationship going with so many miles between them? Would what they felt for one another stand the test of distance and time?

And what, exactly, was it that they felt for one another? Was it love at first sight? Was it what everyone calls, True Love? The sort of love that lasts a lifetime and can overcome anything and everything that is thrown at it. Was it a mixture of love and lust? The kind of love that relies on both parties remaining attracted to one another throughout its duration, but not necessarily strong enough to weather all storms or ignore other temptations. Was it the kind of love that explodes and burns with passion in the early days and then fizzles out and dies after a certain amount of time?

Watching Marian sleep, her long eyelashes flickering every so often as if she was aware of being watched, Parker was sure it was True Love.

He had thought what he had felt for Isabella was True Love, but Isabella had never made him feel like this. He had never considered giving up his dream for Isabella.

She had been upset with him when he had bought *The Dream*. They had even argued about it. Isabella had wanted him to use at least a percentage of the money Jack had left him, to buy a bigger house. They were living in the house that Parker had bought in his early twenties, when he had moved out of his parents' house to get a foot on the property ladder. He had never actually asked Isabella to move in with him, but day by day and week by week, she had.

But even that house was just a means to an end. Parker had originally intended to sell it, when his other savings had accumulated sufficiently, to buy a boat. Jack's bequest meant he had been able to keep the house, and it would be rented out while he sailed the seas. That, to him, was an added bonus. His parents would be handling that while he was away.

And Isabella would be going with him. She knew it was his dream. Being with him meant sharing that dream, together. He only realised the dream was more of a nightmare for her when she had dumped him. He had known she was having doubts about living on a yacht, but it had never occurred to him to tell her he would give up his dream for her. Because the truth was, he never would have.

But now, after only knowing Marian for less than two days, if he had to choose between his dream and Marian, he was seriously considering choosing Marian.

He ran his hands through his hair and cursed beneath his breath.

Why had this had to happen now?

Why couldn't he have met her at the end of the season, not the start?

'Good morning.' She startled him out of his thoughts.

'You're awake! Good morning.' He smiled as she gazed at him. 'Marian ... I've been thinking.'

'Don't think. Kiss me.'

Her voice was like a caress, her smile; an aphrodisiac. Her kiss on his mouth; a jolt that sent blood rushing to every part of him. Her hand gliding downwards over his stomach; a promise of a very good start to the day.

Chapter 30

Marian left Parker in bed and went to make coffee.

'I'll go and do that,' he had said, but she had smiled and shaken her head.

'You need to rest and regain your strength ... for when I return,' she had teased, as she slipped from beneath the duvet, threw on her dressing gown and hurried to the door.

The truth was, she needed to pee, but she did not want to spoil the romance of the moment by saying that.

'You're insatiable,' he said, his eyes dancing with pleasure. 'And incredible. Hurry back.'

She blew him a kiss and softly closed the door. It was early and she did not want to wake the others.

To her surprise, Bel was sitting in the kitchen, on a chair she must have moved across to the window. With the fingers of one hand, she was tracing the rivers of rain running down the pane, and holding a mug in the other. She jumped as Marian entered.

'Good morning, Bel,' Marian said. 'You're up early.'

'Morning.' Bel gave her a tight smile. 'I've made a pot of coffee.' She nodded her head towards the worktop where a large pot of coffee bubbled welcomingly. 'But I owe you a huge apology for last night. Along with a vase. Did I break anything else or was that it? My memory is a bit hazy this morning.'

'You don't owe me anything.' Marian smiled warmly. She got two mugs from the cupboard and poured herself a cup of coffee, leaving the mug for Parker empty for the moment. 'And besides, you've made coffee. That more than makes up for the vase. It wasn't one of my favourites, anyway.'

'Thanks for being so nice. I really am sorry though. I shouldn't have got so drunk and I definitely shouldn't have created a scene when I was a guest in your home.'

'Honestly, Bel. Please don't worry about it. It had obviously been building for a while. It had to come to a head sooner or later. How ... how are you feeling about it all this morning though?'

Bel puffed out a lengthy sigh. 'A bit like someone who has let her own problems and emotions cloud her judgement.' She swivelled round to face Marian. 'Can I be completely honest with you, Marian?'

'Er. Yes. Of course.' Marian was not sure she was the right person for Bel to be 'completely honest' with, or what Bel was about to say, but she could hardly say 'no'.

Bel took a deep breath. 'When my husband left, it hurt me more than I led everyone to believe. And when I was told I wouldn't be able to have kids, I also pretended it wasn't a big deal. I even convinced myself it wasn't. I said as much to you. But the truth is, it is. It's a huge deal. I wanted kids, Marian. I want a family. I want to be in love and to be loved. I want...' She stopped and shook her head.

'I believe most of us want that, Bel. And I know it might not help right now, but you can still be in love and be loved. You can still have a family. I realise adopting a child isn't the same, but there are so many children out there who need loving homes. You could give a child a home, Bel.' Marian hesitated. 'I ... I can't pretend to know how you feel about not being able to have children of your own. But I can understand a little of the pain and torment of losing a child. I ... I'd like to tell you something. If that's okay with you. It's a ... a secret I've kept hidden for years. Only my mum's best friend, Stella knows about it. But

I think it may help you to see that I do know a little of what you have been through. To a very small degree.'

'Are you sure you want to share it with me? I'd like to know, of course. And I'll keep your secret safe. You can count on me on that score.'

Marian nodded slowly. 'I've recently found out that secrets have a way of being discovered no matter how hard, or how well, we think we've kept them hidden. And maybe it's time I shared it anyway.' She put her mug on the worktop. 'I'll just blurt it out. That's easiest. I had a miscarriage when I was seventeen.'

'What? On my god, Marian!'

Marian nodded. 'When my parents died … also when I was seventeen. It was not a good year, I have to say. I can now, sort of, joke about what hell it was. Jokes have often been my way of coping when things get tough. Anyway, I still miss them dreadfully. I always will. Dad died one week before my birthday. Mum, a few months later. I was devastated, obviously. It was as if I was walking around in a fog. I couldn't function normally. I didn't know what day of the week it was. I was a mess. Mum's best friend, Stella was my guardian, and she did – excuse the pun – a *stellar* job, but I was lost and lonely and heartbroken. Clementine Cove is the sort of place a lot of people come to on holiday, believe it or not, and I met a guy...' Marian's voice trailed off as she recalled the deeply hidden memories.

'There's always a guy,' Bel said, smiling wanly. 'So what happened? Did he leave you when you told him about the baby? Like my husband did?'

Marian shook her head. 'He didn't know about the baby. And I didn't know I was pregnant until three months later. We were only together while he was here. We didn't exchange numbers or anything. I wasn't in my right mind because of my grief, so...' Marian shrugged. 'I couldn't believe it when I realised. I told Stella and she said it was my decision. I wanted to keep the baby. Maybe partly because it felt as if I might have a family again. I'd lost my parents but now I had a chance to be someone else's Mum. We kept it secret because Stella wanted me to have time to think things through. I was just beginning to get excited and was thinking of telling people and then ... I had a miscarriage. We decided not to tell anyone. So no one other than Stella knew I was grieving for the child I'd lost in addition to grieving for my parents. Although someone else did find out. But that's another story and it doesn't matter now.'

'Oh, Marian, I'm so sorry.'

'It's okay. It was a long, long time ago. I came to terms with it. Eventually. But that's why I wanted to tell you. Obviously, it's nothing compared to your experience, but I understand the hurt, frustration, anger ... and even guilt, you go through when you miscarry.'

Bel nodded. 'Thanks for sharing that with me. And you're right. I was so hurt, angry, frustrated, and yes, guilty. It's crazy, isn't it? We have nothing to feel guilty for. And yet we do. Anyway, I let all that hurt, anger, frustration and guilt build up inside me and I've been taking it out on my friends. I suppose, in a way, because I knew I could get away with doing that to them.'

'We often hurt those we love the most. And often because we're hurting so badly ourselves.'

Bel topped up her coffee and they sat in silence, each lost in their own thoughts, watching the rain run down the windows and the trees swaying to and fro in the wind.

'But this thing with Jasper,' Bel said, after a while. 'Well ... I also feel like I've finally stood up for myself and stopped something continuing, that to me, was becoming really unpleasant and upsetting. Does that make sense?'

'Yes. It does.'

'Nikki, Jasper and I had a really good talk last night. An honest and open, no holds barred kind of talk. And I think ... I hope, Jasper and I are okay. I would hate to lose his friendship. But then again, I couldn't let him believe it was okay for him to do what he was doing because, rightly or wrongly, what he was doing was really upsetting me.'

'You had every right to say what you said. It was a difficult situation, but I don't think you'll lose his friendship. I do think he might walk on eggshells around you for a while though. But that's not a bad thing. You can establish new boundaries and then I'm sure your friendship will be on a good footing once again.'

'I hope so. And I hope Parker's not too cross with me, but I'm pretty sure he won't be. He's one of the nicest guys I've ever known. Oh. How was your night?' Bel grinned suddenly. 'Or don't you kiss and tell?'

Marian smiled. 'I don't kiss and tell. But I will say one thing. It was even better than I expected it to be.'

'Good for you.' Bel looked genuinely pleased. 'I think us having to come to Clementine Cove to shelter from the storm was the best thing that could've happened for Parker. And maybe not just for him. For all of us. But more so for him.'

'You do? Why?'

Bel rolled her eyes. 'If you had seen how upset he was about Isabella and Greg, you wouldn't need to ask me that question. You talked about Jasper walking on eggshells, well, we all thought we'd be doing that all summer, with Parker. We thought it would take him ages to get over Isabella. To move on. It seems we were all wrong. It's as if he's forgotten who Isabella is. As is she never existed. As if the woman never smashed his heart to bits.' She shook her head and laughed. 'It's unbelievable, actually. But meeting you has been like a fresh start for him.'

Marian contemplated Bel's words, taking several slow sips of what was left of her coffee.

On the one hand, those comments had been music to Marian's ears. To think that, after meeting her, Parker had forgotten his heartbreak and the woman who had caused it. That was monumental.

On the other hand, Parker would be leaving soon. Didn't that mean he would experience heartbreak for a second time? Or at the very least, heartache?

Or did it?

Hadn't Bel also previously said that Marian might be *the rebound*?

In that scenario, Parker would be able to leave and have no regrets. It would be Marian who would be left broken hearted.

'You don't seem pleased.' Bel interrupted Marian's thoughts. 'Have I said the wrong thing?'

'No. Um. It's just that ... He'll be leaving once the weather clears. You all will. As wonderful as this has been – and it has, believe me – it'll be over. I'll be standing on the jetty pretty soon, waving you all goodbye as you sail off into the sunset. And that's the way it has to be. I know that. I'm glad I got to meet him. I'm glad I got to meet you all. But Parker has his dream. And I've got my business. Which I'm really looking forward to getting back on its feet. With Archer's help. It's all very exciting. I can't wait to get things moving. Meeting Parker ... and all of you, has been fun. A lovely distraction when I really needed it. Perfect timing, in fact. Both for Parker and for me. But our paths lead in different directions, so that's that. And it's okay. This ... whatever it was between us wasn't meant to last. It was just ... another holiday fling. But this time, it won't have any unforeseen consequences. 'Everything happens for a reason', my mum always said. Perhaps meeting me has helped Parker to realise he can move on from Isabella. And meeting him has shown me I wasn't in love with Archer. Not in the way I thought. I was just lonely and depressed because my business was failing. But now, Archer, Bentley and I have such fabulous plans, and the future's looking bright. I couldn't be happier.'

She was rambling and she knew it, and Bel was looking at her very oddly. Very oddly indeed.

'Er. Okay,' Bel said, and then she raised her brows. 'Morning Parker! I didn't see you standing there.'

Chapter 31

The storm quickly subsided. Less than an hour after Parker joined Marian and Bel in the kitchen, the wind died down to little more than a breeze; it was drizzling intermittently rather than raining, and glimpses of sunshine peeped out from behind the rapidly dispersing clouds.

Marian's happiness had faded even faster.

She did not know how much of her and Bel's conversation Parker had overheard, but when Bel had spotted him, standing in the doorway, bare chested and only wearing the Boxer shorts Marian had stripped off him last night, he had not looked pleased. And he seemed to hesitate at the open door as if he was not sure whether to join them, or to walk in the opposite direction.

What was it with these people and doorways? Every time Marian turned round, one or more of them seemed to be hovering, either watching or listening.

'Sorry,' Marian had said, smiling at Parker, albeit a little anxiously. 'You must've thought I'd gone to Kenya to get your coffee. Bel and I started chatting.'

'Yes,' he said, without a hint of that crooked smile anywhere to be seen. 'So I gathered.'

'There's coffee in the pot,' Bel said. 'And I want to apologise for last night.'

'Last night?' he repeated, the crease between his brows suggesting he had no idea what Bel was referring to.

'The scene I caused. Well, strictly speaking it was Jasper who caused it. Or maybe a bit of both. Anyway. I'm sorry.'

Parker shrugged. 'It's Marian you should apologise to, not me.'

'Been there, done that.' Bel grinned.

'I'll get you that coffee.' Marian filled the mug she had got out earlier and he took it from her without the slightest smile.

'Thanks,' was all he said.

Bel frowned at him. 'Er. Is everything okay? Only you look a little … lost. Did you forget where you left your trousers?' She winked at Marian.

'No,' he said. 'I'm going to have a shower, if that's okay.' He glanced at Marian for a split second and then looked directly at Bel.

'With any luck we should be able to leave before lunchtime. I just checked the app on my phone and the forecast is good. The last of this weather should have cleared by mid-morning at the latest.'

'Oh!' Marian and Bel said in unison and looked at one another.

'So soon?' Marian croaked.

'Yeah,' said Bel. 'Why the rush?'

'What's the point in delaying? The sooner we leave, the sooner we'll arrive at our destination.'

'But I...' Marian let her words trail off.

What could she say?

But I thought you were going to stay. I thought we were going to have sex again this morning. I thought you had feelings for me.

How could she say any of those things?

She had known this was coming. She had known he would be leaving. She had just said precisely that to Bel, less than five minutes ago.

But she had not expected him to be leaving quite so soon. And definitely not before lunchtime.

'Tell the others, would you?' Parker instructed Bel. 'We'll head to *The Dream* in half an hour or so. We can have breakfast on board and carry out a thorough check to make sure there was no storm damage. And then we'll say our goodbyes and we'll be on our way. Thanks for everything, Marian.'

He turned and marched away before his words had sunk in.

'What ... what just happened?' Marian asked, casting Bel a pleading look.

Bel shook her head slowly as though she was as perplexed as Marian was by Parker's tone and behaviour.

'Search me,' said Bel, looking thoughtful now. 'But he was just like this the day we left Broadlands Bay. The day Isabella and Greg were getting married. He told us he had to leave before the bells of St Benedict's rang out. Now, it seems, we have to leave Clementine Cove before lunch. But quite why that is, I have absolutely no idea.'

Chapter 32

Marian tried to talk to Parker, but he avoided her.

When he got out of the shower and saw her waiting for him, he told her he was cold and needed to get dressed.

When she reached out for him, he darted out of her way.

When she blocked his exit from the bedroom by placing her outstretched arms across the threshold, he had no choice but to listen to what she had to say.

'Have I done something wrong?' she asked, trying hard not to let tears of hurt and frustration well up in her eyes.

'No.'

'Then why are you leaving in such a hurry?'

'The storm's over.'

'So that's it? Just like that?'

He shrugged. 'I don't know what you're trying to say. We both knew I would be leaving as soon as the weather cleared.'

'Yes. But I didn't realise you'd rush off the minute the last cloud blew away. I thought you'd ... at least take some time to say goodbye.'

'How long does it take to say goodbye?'

'I suppose that depends on how eager you are to leave.'

Marian was getting angry now. Less than an hour ago they'd been having incredible sex, with the promise of more to come. He had said he couldn't keep his hands off her. He had said he wanted to stay. He'd been passionate, tender and loving. Now he didn't want to touch her and was as cold, hard and as unfeeling as a block of ice.

'There's no point in staying, as I said.'

He didn't even want to look at her, it seemed. His eyes darted in all directions except towards her.

Had everything he had said been a lie? And if so, why?

She could not understand what was happening. Her head was spinning. Her stomach was churning. Her legs could hardly hold her upright. Her breath seemed to be stuck in her chest. Was she having a panic attack of some sort?

Or was this all from lack of sleep? She had had virtually no sleep for the last two nights. The first, because she had spent most of it thinking about having sex with Parker; the second, because she *was* having sex with Parker. Incredible sex. The best sex she had ever had. Not that she had had that much. There had been very few relationships in Marian's life.

But no man had ever treated her like this.

Was this because of something Parker had overheard her and Bel discussing in the kitchen? Had he heard her tell Bel about her own miscarriage?

But why would that make him behave so coldly towards her?

'I ... I thought you liked me, Parker,' she mumbled.

'Yes.' He cleared his throat. 'I did. But it's time for me to go. I ... I hope things go well with your business and that your plans with Archer and Bentley all work out.'

She felt deflated. Like a discarded balloon the day after the best birthday party ever.

'Thanks.'

'And thank you. It was very kind of you to let us stay here. Now if you'll excuse me, I'd better get to *The Dream* and check she's fit to sail.'

Marian limply stepped aside, but she reached out for him as he walked past her.

'Parker! I don't understand. Was everything that happened between us, especially last night, just your way of passing time?'

Something flashed across his eyes. Warmth? Tenderness? Regret? Replaced with cold indifference.

'At the end of the day, it was just sex, wasn't it, Marian? We both wanted one another. We both enjoyed last night. Now it's time to go our separate ways.'

'Will I ... will I ever see you again?'

'If I need a safe harbour in a storm, who knows?' His smile was as icy as his voice.

How dare he? The bastard!

'Well. Thanks for that. I ... No. It doesn't matter. Have a safe voyage, Parker. I hope your dream lives up to your expectations. Goodbye.'

Somehow, she managed to walk the length of the hall without crying, without looking back, even when she thought she heard him say her name. She reached the stairs and ran down them without caring if she tripped. Luckily, she didn't. She raced to the door and slammed it behind her, bumping into Archer as she spun round.

'Hey, Marian! Where's the fire?'

'Archer!'

'Where're you off to in ... What's wrong? Has something happened?' Archer placed his hands gently on her shoulders. 'Don't cry!' He eased her into the comfort of his arms. 'Let's go back inside and you can tell me what's upset you.'

'No!' she sobbed into his shoulder. 'Not in there. *He's* in there. And I never want to see that man again for as long as I live!'

Chapter 33

Should he go after her? Parker hesitated halfway along the hall.

She had seemed upset. Almost as upset as he was. But she had not stopped when he had called after her and she had run down the stairs as if the place was on fire.

Perhaps he should not have been quite so cold. Quite so heartless.

Heartless? Hmph! That was a laugh.

Heartbroken more like. And he had not thought that was possible, again. Not after Isabella. Not after he had been adamant that he would not get involved with anyone else for a long time.

And how the hell had he done that, anyway? Fallen for Marian so fast and so hard. He had only known the bloody woman for two days! How was it possible to feel like this? How was it possible to feel so much? Why had he been so hurt, so physically sick almost when he had heard her say those things to Bel in the kitchen?

But what if he had not heard them? Then he would be even more heartbroken, wouldn't he? And he would look like an utter fool. Which is clearly what he was.

What a bloody idiot he had been. To think he had actually considered asking Bel, Nikki and Jasper if maybe they could stay in Clementine Cove for a while. At least until they were due to welcome their first clients on board in the Med. And that wasn't until April. He could have stayed here until April.

Yeah right. Marian would have laughed at that, wouldn't she? Or, worse still, she might have bloody well asked him to leave. How humiliating would that have been?

He had certainly misjudged her, hadn't he? He had seriously been considering delaying his dream just to spend more time with her, and then ... oh yes, that would've been hysterical, wouldn't it? He was actually going to ask her if she would spend some time in the Med – with him.

Shit! It was a bloody good thing he had gone to see what was keeping her this morning. He wouldn't have overheard what she had said to Bel, if he had waited for her in bed.

Waited for her in bed! Hmph. He had genuinely thought she was coming back. He had believed that she felt the same about him as he sodding well felt about her. What a bloody fool. What a jerk. What an idiot. How could he have been so stupid?

What was it she had said? He could not remember it word for word; he had been too shocked to take it in at first as he had walked towards the open door. But he did remember the first words he had heard. And they had felt like a slap across his face.

'Meeting Parker ... and all of you, has been fun. A lovely distraction when I really needed it. Perfect timing, in fact.'

Yeah right. Perfect bloody timing!

And then she had said something along the lines of: 'Our paths lead in different directions. And it's okay. Whatever it was between us wasn't meant to last. It was just another holiday fling.'

Holiday fling? That was all it had been to her. She had used the word 'another', so he clearly wasn't the only one. Well okay. He would tell her that was all it had been to him. He would not let her see how hurt he was. How deeply her words had cut into him.

But what had she meant by that other comment? The one about unforeseen consequences. What were her exact words?

'But this time, it won't have any unforeseen consequences.'

What the hell did that mean? What unforeseen consequences?

All sorts of scenarios popped into his head. And not one of them was pleasant. Just how many holiday flings had Marian had? Had it become a habit? She'd definitely had more than one. Perhaps there had been hundreds.

And yet she had not seemed like the sort of woman who had sex with lots of guys just for fun. No strings attached. Love them and leave them. Well not love, of course. Just sex.

Iris was that type. That had been pretty clear. Not that there was anything wrong with that. He knew lots of guys who did the same. Guys who played the field and had a good time without their feelings ever being involved.

But he was not one of those guys. He had never slept with a woman unless he had feelings for her. Genuine feelings. Maybe not love; not right away, but the start of something that could lead somewhere. And he had thought Marian was the same.

Her words had told him he was wrong.

But it was not the number of flings that bothered him; it was the fact that that was all he had been to her. A fling. And he had wanted so much more. He had wanted a future with her.

'Perhaps meeting me has helped Parker to realise he can move on from Isabella,' she had said. 'And meeting him has shown me I wasn't in love with Archer. Not in the way I thought. I was just lonely and depressed because my business was failing. But now, Archer, Bentley and I have such fabulous plans, and the future's looking bright. I couldn't be happier.'

She was excited about her future. A future that clearly did not include him.

And she had told Bel that she couldn't be happier about that.

Chapter 34

'I thought I might find you here.' Bel said, as she joined Marian at a table in The Bow and Quiver. 'Are you okay?'

Marian merely shrugged in reply.

Bel gave her a wry smile. 'At least you're not in flood of tears, so that's a good thing, isn't it?' She sat on a chair opposite Marian.

'You should've been here an hour ago. Archer nearly drowned.'

Marian was only half joking. When Archer had suggested that if she didn't want to go back inside Cove Café, they should go to his pub to talk, instead, she was sobbing like an overflowing gutter.

Thankfully, the pub was empty; Elodie was still upstairs in bed, and Bentley and the pub staff had not yet arrived.

Archer had insisted Marian drink a glass of brandy, despite the fact that it was only a little after 8 a.m. and whether it was the alcohol, or Archer's comforting arms and equally comforting words, Marian soon felt a great deal better. And then Archer had insisted on cooking her breakfast, but in the pub kitchen so as not to wake Elodie. After that they had chatted about his plans for Cove Café and for Bentley's restaurant, which would be a Café Bistro.

Bel grinned now. 'And you've got your sense of humour back, I see. Where's Archer? Gone to get dry clothes?'

Marian chuckled at that. 'He's popped upstairs to check on Elodie, and to let her know I'm here. I didn't want to go up.' She shook her head. 'Selfishly, a happy, loved up couple isn't really what I need to see right now.'

'Right.' Bel reached into her pocket and handed Marian a piece of paper, with a phone number and an email address written on it. 'That's my number, and that's my email. Don't be a stranger, okay?'

Marian was both surprised and touched. 'Thanks, Bel. Let me give you mine in exchange. Oh. Except I haven't got my bag. Or a pen. Or my phone, so I can't even text it to you. But I will do it later. I'd like to keep in touch.'

'Me too. I feel I've made a new friend.'

'Yes. I feel the same.' Marian gave her a brief smile. 'So ... you are all leaving then? This morning?'

Bel nodded. 'It seems we are. Just a few final checks and then we'll up anchor. Listen, Marian. I'm not sure what's going on in Parker's head, because he won't talk to me about it, but I do know one thing, he–'

Marian raised a hand to stop her. 'Please don't, Bel. I think he made his feelings pretty clear. Or should I say, absence of feelings? Anyway. Please don't make excuses for him.'

'I wasn't going to. I was going to give you an explanation.'

'Doesn't that amount to the same thing? Were you going to tell me that he isn't really over Isabella yet? That this happened too soon. That he needs time to think.'

Bel frowned. 'Y-es. But I was also going to say that...' Bel let her voice trail off when Marian raised her hand again. Bel shrugged and got to her feet. 'Okay. I tried. Don't think too badly of him, Marian.'

'I don't plan to think of him at all.' Marian huffed out a short breath, and managed a smile. 'Please say goodbye to Nikki and Jasper for me. Tell them, if they are ever back this way, to pop in and say hello. And the same goes for you, of course.'

'Thanks. I'll tell them. They were going to come with me, but Parker's in a bit of a mood. He only let me come back to shore because I told him I had to say goodbye to Bentley, and that if he didn't let me, I'd jump ship.' She smiled. 'Good luck with all the plans for your business. You can let me know how it's all going.'

'Thanks. Safe voyage. And happy sailing around the Med. I hope your clients aren't too demanding. You can let me know all the gossip.'

Bel laughed. 'There'll be a lot of that.' She gave Marian a wave. 'Say goodbye to Bentley for me, will you? I texted him to say I'd be here, but he's held up in traffic. There's been an accident at some roundabout. Moneymaker Circle, I think he said. It's not serious but apparently the roads are completely jammed and a lorry has jack-knifed blocking two of the turn-offs. I daren't keep Parker waiting. He might decide to sail off without me and find a replacement chef in Antibes. Not that they'd be a patch on me.'

'Of course they wouldn't. I'll tell Bentley, don't worry.'

'Bye then. You take care.'

Marian nodded. 'You too.' It was almost as if Bel didn't want to go. 'Are you okay, Bel? You're not ... you're not worried about being on the boat with Jasper, are you?'

'What?' Bel shook her head. 'No. Well … maybe a bit. But that's not it. That's not what I'm worried about.'

'What is it then? You know you can tell me anything.'

'I thought I could. But you won't let me! You know what? I'm just going to say it. And you can hold your hand in the air as high as you like, but it needs to be said. I'm worried that you and that moron, Parker are about to make the worst decisions of your lives.'

Chapter 35

'Shit!' Parker had looked everywhere. 'Where the hell is my bloody phone?'

'Search me,' Jasper shrugged. 'But not literally, man. I haven't hidden it up my arse or anything.'

Parker tutted and pulled a face; Nikki burst out laughing.

'Now there's an image I'll have trouble getting out of my head,' she said. 'When and where did you last see it? And I don't mean Jasper's arse. I mean your phone.'

Parker frowned and made a low growl.

'How the hell do I know? I had it when I checked the forecast at ... earlier.' He didn't want to say her name. He didn't even want to think about her. But all morning, despite needing to get *The Dream* ready to sail, he had done nothing else *but think* about the bloody woman. He cleared his throat. 'I'm sure I had it when we came on board. I'm almost certain I put it on the table in the dinette when we were eating breakfast. But I don't recall having it after that. I've searched high and low and I can't find it anywhere. And where in God's name is Bel? She said she'd only be thirty minutes. Forty-five at the most. It's been...' he glanced at his watch. 'Oh okay. Twenty minutes. It feels like longer.'

'It feels like a life sentence to me and Jasper,' Nikki said. 'If you're going to be this bloody stroppy all the way to the Med, you might not have a crew by the time we get there. I thought you were pissed about Isabella, but this is beyond anything I've...' Nikki raised her brows. 'Okay. I'll shut up. But you're not going to win yachting personality of the year, believe me.'

Jasper took his own phone out of his back pocket and held it in front of Parker.

'Don't you have a phone tracker app? I've got one on mine. It lets you see where your phone is in case someone steals it. Or you leave it somewhere. Look.'

'Thanks. That's really helpful.' Parker frowned at him. 'Just call me, will you?'

'But ... I thought you didn't have your phone?'

'Oh for God's sake! Call my phone. That way we might be able to hear where it is.'

'Hey, man. No need to shout. I'll call it. There. See. It's ringing.'

Everyone was silent, but Parker could not hear his ring tone.

'We need to walk around and see if we can find it. You go that way, Nikki. I'll go this. Keep ringing it, Jasper.'

'A *please*, would be nice,' Nikki said.

'It's gone to voicemail,' said Jasper, and then he winked at Nikki. 'Want me to leave a message?'

Jasper and Nikki sniggered, and Parker stormed off in search of his phone.

Chapter 36

'Is that person on the jetty waving at us?' Bel said. 'Oh. It looks like Marian.'

'Marian!' Parker was halfway down the stairs to the lower deck but he turned and ran to look, and then he checked himself.

The last person he wanted to look at now, was Marian.

He had been about to continue searching for his phone, having asked Bel if she had seen it, the moment she had returned.

'Not for a while, no,' Bel had said.

'Aww,' said Nikki now, carrying a tray with four mugs of coffee. 'She's probably come to wave us off. That's nice. Let me see.' She put the tray down and waved back.

'Who're we waving to?' Jasper asked, coming to get his coffee. 'And why are we having coffee up here?'

Nikki glanced at him. 'Bel told me to bring it to the bridge. And we're waving at Marian. Look.'

Jasper looked. And then he grinned as Parker headed back towards the stairs.

'Parker?'

'What?'

'You know before, when Marian was waving and pointing and holding something to her ear during the storm?'

'Yes. So what?'

'And she had your phone, right? And you've lost your phone, yes? Well, I'm not certain, man, but I think Marian may have found it.'

Parker nearly lost his balance on the top step, but he managed to find his footing.

'She can't have. That's ... that's not possible.' He slowly made his way back to the window and looked out. 'I had it here, on this yacht, this morning. I haven't been back to shore since. How can my phone have possibly...?' He stared at Bel. 'Bel!'

'Yes, Parker?' She smiled at him.

'Is there something you want to tell me?'

She looked thoughtful. 'No, Parker.'

'Are you sure?'

Bel nodded.

'Then how did Marian get my phone?'

Bel raised her brows. 'Perhaps you left it at her place. You know? Like you did the last time.'

He shook his head slowly and decisively. 'I did not leave it at ... anywhere. I had it here this morning. The only way my phone could be in Marian's hand right now is if someone gave it to her.'

Bel gasped. 'I can promise you, hand on heart, I did not give Marian your phone.'

'Then how could she have got it?'

'Is it your phone though?' Nikki asked. 'Here. Borrow mine and call it. If it is yours, she'll answer it.'

'It's locked.' Parker said. 'She can't.'

'I've got Marian's phone number,' Bel said. 'Oh. But because she ran out this morning, in tears, I might add, she probably didn't take her phone.'

'In tears?' Parker's chest tightened. 'She ... she was in tears?'

'Uh-huh.'

He frowned at Bel. 'How do you know that? You weren't there when she ran away. I mean, left.'

Bel sighed. 'No. But I've just been talking to her in the pub. And believe me, Parker. She was upset. Genuinely upset. But of course you're not interested in Marian, are you?'

He glowered at her. 'You've got that the wrong way round. She's not interested in me.'

'Really? I think you're the one who's got it wrong. But that doesn't solve the problem with your phone, does it? And there's only one way to do that. You need to get in the tender and go and see her.'

'Why do *I* have to go?'

'Because it's your phone, you moron.' Bel smiled.

'I'm confused,' Jasper said. 'How did Marian get Parker's phone?'

'It really doesn't matter,' said Bel, sighing. 'All that matters is that Marian's there and Parker's here and the only way he'll get his phone, is if he goes and gets it.'

Chapter 37

She could leave it on the jetty. Now that they had seen her waving and Parker was in the tender heading towards the shore, she could leave his phone and run. She wouldn't have to see him face to face if she did that. She wouldn't have to hear his voice, or look into his eyes, or wish that crooked smile would creep across his mouth.

Yes. That was the best thing to do.

She would wave it in the air once again and then she would point to the deck of the jetty. He would realise what she meant. Better still, she could leave it on the steps. That way he could probably reach out and grab his phone without even getting out of the tender.

She went down the first two steps and checked how high the water came. She would leave his phone on the one above the water level, which was five steps down due to the tide. If she left it on step four, it would be safe there. Now the weather was so much better, the water in the bay was calm and there was hardly as much as a ripple. She waved the phone in the air and made sure Parker was looking. And then she pointed to the step. She saw him shake his head but she ignored that. She put the phone safely on the fourth step down and then pointed at it again. Then she turned and ran back up the steps.

'Marian! Wait!'

Her heart thumped in her chest and for a second, she wasn't sure what to do. Stay, and have the chance to see him one last time, or run away as fast as she could, and never see him again. Those were the options and she was torn. She did a half turn on the spot, and then turned back, but she misjudged her footing.

'Marian!'

She reached out for the jetty post but it was too far from her fingers and she screamed his name as she tumbled backwards and thudded into the water.

The weight of her clothes, her boots and her coat all pulled her down. Not that it was very deep, especially with the tide out. She knew that. In fact, if she put her feet down instead of thrashing about, she could probably stand on the shingle bottom.

Before she had a chance to do so, she realised she was being hauled out of the water.

Seconds later, she was in his arms. Parker's arms. And he was kissing her head and her face and calling her name and hugging her all at once.

'Marian! Are you okay? Are you hurt? Oh my God! You could've drowned. I might've lost you. Marian! Speak to me.'

She coughed up a mouthful of water she must've swallowed, and tried to wriggle her face free from his tight embrace.

'Parker! I can't breathe. Please don't hold me so tight.'

'Shit. I'm sorry! Are you okay?'

She gently pushed him away and smiled.

'I'm fine. And I wouldn't have drowned. The water here isn't that deep. I could've touched the seabed with my feet, if you hadn't hauled me out. But thank you.' She shivered. 'God! That water was cold.'

'We need to get you warm and dry. Right now.' He glanced towards Cove Café and then towards his yacht. '*The Dream*'s closer. I think we should go there.'

'Wait!'

'Why? You need to get out of those clothes, Marian.'

'I know I do. But your phone's still on the step.' She saw him hesitate. 'If you leave it there, a seagull will probably take it. And I would've almost drowned for nothing.'

She managed a smile and her heart skipped a beat as he gave her a small smile back.

He took off his jacket and hurriedly wrapped it around her, and then skilfully manoeuvred the tender so that he could reach out and retrieve his phone. He was just in time. A seagull swooped down and almost took it from him.

'I told you so,' she said, snuggling into his jacket. 'How did your phone come to be in the pub?'

He shoved the phone in the back pocket of his jeans and headed towards *The Dream*.

'I was going to ask you that.'

'Me? I haven't got a clue. I just heard it ringing and when I looked, it was sitting on a chair, right beside where Bel had sat about ten minutes before. I assumed it was hers until I saw the photo of you and your family.'

'I knew it,' he said.

'What?'

He looked at her in silence for a couple of seconds.

'It doesn't matter. Are you warmer now?'

She nodded. 'A little. But I've just realised. We should've gone back to my place. Now you'll have to take me back to shore again before you can leave.'

'I know. That's not important. What's important is to get you warm and dry as quickly as possible.'

When he had hauled her out of the freezing water, she was so happy to see him that she didn't feel the cold. Or the shock. But now, hunched up beneath his jacket, cold crept over her like a shroud and chilled her to the bone. But she wouldn't tell Parker that. She had a feeling he would worry and there was no point in that. He was going as fast as he could.

The journey to the yacht did not take very long; a matter of minutes at most. Bel was waiting with towels, Nikki brought her a hot drink, and Jasper handed Parker a blanket to wrap around her.

'I'll stow the tender,' Jasper said. 'Welcome aboard, Marian. Are you okay?'

'F-fine thanks. Just c-cold'

Bel dabbed at her with a towel while Marian took a sip of the tea Nikki gave her but she shrieked when Parker swept her into his arms.

'I can walk!'

'Not in those boots. Not on my deck.'

'It's a rule on boats,' Bel said, taking the cup from her and following behind them as Parker carried Marian along the deck and up a flight of stairs. 'Heels can do considerable damage to the wooden deck and the soles can make scuff marks that can be really hard to remove.'

'Of c-course. Sorry. I f-forgot. But c-couldn't I have just t-taken off my b-boots?'

'We will,' Parker said, standing her down on what looked like a very expensive rug beside a king size bed, in what she saw was a large and rather opulent cabin.

Bel placed another of the towels on the bed and, with the blanket still wrapped around her and also Parker's jacket, he sat Marian onto the bed, holding her arms gently as he did so.

'Take off your clothes,' he instructed, kneeling down to remove her boots.

Tingles ran up and down her and it wasn't because of the cold.

'And they s-say r-romance is d-dead,' she joked.

He met her eyes for one second and then he stood up.

'Perhaps Bel should help you.'

'Yes. P-perhaps she s-should.'

'Fine.' He looked undecided. 'She needs to get in the shower asap, Bel.'

'I know.'

'And then get her into bed.'

'Parker!'

'Okay. I'm going.' He cast a concerned glance at Marian. 'You are sure you're all right, aren't you? You didn't hit your head or anything.'

'I'm fine. H-honestly.'

'Call me if you need me.'

'Well,' said Bel, when Parker had left. 'That didn't quite go to plan.' She beamed at Marian. 'But I think this might be even better.'

'Plan? What p-plan?'

'Don't worry about it, Marian. Just leave it with me. Now, let's get you in that shower.'

It didn't take much time for Marian to warm up once she had had a shower and got dressed in some of Bel's clothes. Even so, Parker insisted on her wearing one of his jumpers, and he made her get into bed. Not that she was complaining. It was an extremely comfortable bed.

'Get some rest,' he said, when he brought her another cup of tea.

'I don't need rest,' she replied. 'It's not even midday. And besides, I need to get back to shore so that you can leave by lunchtime.'

'We're not leaving at lunchtime.'

'Oh? Why not? Don't delay on my account.'

'I'm not. I'm delaying on mine. Now drink your tea.'

'Don't keep telling me what to do, Parker!'

'Fine. But don't try to get up or I'll carry you right back here again.'

She gasped. 'You can't manhandle me just because you feel like it. Didn't that scene with Bel and Jasper teach you anything?'

'Believe me, Marian, the last thing I feel like doing is manhandling you.'

'Or anything else. I know! You made that pretty clear. Although you seemed more than happy to have mad, passionate sex with me when the weather was bad. But the minute the sun comes out, you're off.'

'What! What *are* you talking about?'

'You! One minute you're telling me how gorgeous you think I am. How sexy. How much you want me. How you don't want to leave. The next, it's as if I've got ... scurvy or something. You don't want to touch me, or look at me and you certainly don't want to kiss me or have sex with me again.'

His jaw dropped as he stared at her, listening to what she said. And then his eyes narrowed and his temper flared.

'Are you insane? All I've wanted to do since almost the moment we met is to kiss you. And to make love with you. I was even stupid enough to consider asking the others if we could stay on for a while. And even more ridiculously, I was actually hoping you might come out and join me in the Med. Hmph! I'm obviously the one who's insane, aren't I?

Insane for believing that you felt for me even half of what I feel for you. But no. You saw this as just a holiday fling. Oh. Sorry. *Another* holiday fling. You're the one who doesn't want to kiss *me* or have sex with *me* again. You can't wait to get on with your new and exciting plans for your business. You're the one who said meeting us had been fun. A lovely distraction when you really needed it. Perfect timing. I heard you say that, Marian. I heard you say your future's looking bright and you couldn't be happier. A future in which I have no place. No place at all.'

Marian stared at him in astonishment.

'Wh-what else did you hear?'

'What else? You mean there was more? Great. But I think I heard enough, thanks. I thought Isabella had smashed my heart to pieces, but I was wrong. You did that, Marian. And I still can't believe it is possible.'

'So ... the reason you were as cold as ice to me was ... because you thought I saw us as a holiday fling? That I didn't have feelings for you? Is that what you're telling me?'

'I heard you say those things, Marian.' He glared at her.

'Yes. Completely out of context. I was trying to convince myself that I would be okay once you'd left. As for the rest. Well, I'd need to tell you the entire conversation for you to understand all that. And I don't have time for that right now.'

She pushed back the duvet and swung her legs out of the bed.

'If you think you can just up and leave, you can think again. You're going to stay here until I'm sure you're fully recovered. You might have delayed shock or ... Marian? What're doing?'

She had taken his hands in hers and was leading him back to the bed.

'What do you think I'm doing, Parker? I'm going to show you that this is not a holiday fling. I'm going to show you just how much I want to kiss you and make love with you. And ... if you'll let me, I'm going to show you just how much I want you to be in my future. And I don't even care where that future is. Here, the Med. On Mars. All I care about is being with you. I love you, Parker. As crazy as that might be. And I'm not going to let you go anywhere. At least, not without me.'

'You ... you love me?' His brows furrowed in disbelief.

And then she kissed him, deeply and passionately.

After a time, he eased her away and looked her in the eyes. 'You love me!' He lifted her in the air and swung her round and round. 'I love you too, Marian. And yes, maybe it is crazy. But I don't care. I've never felt like this before.'

She smiled down at him. 'Not even with Isabella?'

'Who's Isabella?'

He beamed at her as he slowly lowered her feet back to the floor and then he swept her up in his arms and carried her the short distance to the bed.

Chapter 38

One week later, Marian wiped the white swirly writing from the 'Specials' blackboard on the wall of Cove Café and smiled. The sensation overwhelmed her. All the worry, fear and doubt, especially of the last few months, had melted away, like the marshmallows in her special hot chocolate.

Yes, some people might think she was crazy. Some might say she would regret her decision. But she knew, deep down, she wouldn't. Every fibre of her being told her that this was the right choice.

Archer had been wonderful, as Marian had known he would be. He would look after not just Cove Café while she was gone but also the rest of her cottage. And when he and Elodie were in Australia, Bentley would step in.

As she turned the sign on the pink front door to Closed, even though she felt a slight twinge that this was the last time she would touch this sign for many months to come, she also felt euphoric.

'Everything happens for a reason,' her mum had always said, along with, 'Ask the Universe, and it will provide.'

Well, her mum had been right, and the Universe had excelled itself.

Her mum had also said that when Marian found a man she loved, who loved her as much as her parents had loved one another, she should never let him go.

Marian had found that man in Parker. And he wasn't going anywhere – without her.

She would return, possibly in September, or maybe in October. Or perhaps they would sail to the Caribbean and spend the winter there, returning to Clementine Cove next summer.

Their plans for the future were fluid at the moment, other than spending this season in the Med, along with Bel and Nikki and Jasper. It meant Jasper offering to give up his bunk so that Marian could sleep there with Parker, but Jasper was more than happy to sleep on the long bench seat in the dinette.

Besides, it was only when the clients who had pre-booked Parker's master suite were on board. Now Parker wasn't taking any new bookings for that, so he and Marian would have the luxury of a king size bed for at least part of the season.

'Ready?' Parker said, reaching out his hand and taking Marian's in his.

'Ready,' she said, smiling up at him.

He kissed her tenderly and when he eased away from her, he looked into her eyes.

'No regrets?'

'Yes. One.' She smiled at his expression of concern. 'That if I had known I only had to ask, and the Universe would send you to me, I would've asked it to send you much, much sooner.'

Coming soon

Please see my website for details.
www.emilyharvale.com

You can sign up for my newsletter while you're there, and also play book related games and puzzles in the Games Room of my Open House.

A Note from Emily

A little piece of my heart goes into every one of my books and when I send them on their way, I really hope they bring a smile to someone's face. If this book made you smile, or gave you a few pleasant hours of relaxation, I'd love you to tell your friends.

And if you have a minute or two to post a review (just a few words will do) or even simply a rating, that would be lovely too. Reviews help other readers choose an author's books, which is why we're always asking you lovely readers to do them. Huge thanks to those of you who do so, and for your wonderful comments and support on social media. Thank you.

A writer's life can be lonely at times. Sharing a virtual cup of coffee or a glass of wine, or exchanging a few friendly words via my website Open House, or on Facebook, Twitter or Instagram is so much fun.

You can sign up for my newsletter too. It's absolutely free, your email address is safe and won't be shared and I won't bombard you, I promise. You can enter competitions and enjoy some giveaways. In addition to that, there's my author page on Facebook.

There's also my lovely, Facebook group and now my wonderful, Emily's Open House (both mentioned earlier) where you'll find free book-related games and puzzles, meet me, and other fans, and get access to my book news, sometimes early extracts from my books and lots more besides. You'll find all my contact links on my website and in the Contact section in this book. Hope to chat with you soon.

I can't wait to bring you more stories that I hope will capture your heart, mind and imagination, allowing you to escape into a world of romance in some enticingly beautiful settings.

To see all my books, please go to the books page on my website.

Also by Emily Harvale

The Golf Widows' Club
Sailing Solo
Carole Singer's Christmas
Christmas Wishes
A Slippery Slope
The Perfect Christmas Plan
Be Mine
It Takes Two
Bells and Bows on Mistletoe Row

Lizzie Marshall series:
Highland Fling – book 1
Lizzie Marshall's Wedding – book 2

Goldebury Bay series:
Ninety Days of Summer – book 1
Ninety Steps to Summerhill – book 2
Ninety Days to Christmas – book 3

Hideaway Down series:
A Christmas Hideaway – book 1
Catch A Falling Star – book 2
Walking on Sunshine – book 3
Dancing in the Rain – book 4

Hall's Cross series
Deck the Halls – book 1
The Starlight Ball – book 2

Michaelmas Bay series
Christmas Secrets in Snowflake Cove – book 1
Blame it on the Moonlight – book 2

Lily Pond Lane series
The Cottage on Lily Pond Lane – four-part serial
Part One – New beginnings
Part Two – Summer secrets
Part Three – Autumn leaves
Part Four – Trick or treat
Christmas on Lily Pond Lane
Return to Lily Pond Lane
A Wedding on Lily Pond Lane
Secret Wishes and Summer Kisses on Lily Pond Lane

Wyntersleap series
Christmas at Wynter House – Book 1
New Beginnings at Wynter House – Book 2
A Wedding at Wynter House – Book 3
Love is in the Air – spin off

Merriment Bay series
Coming Home to Merriment Bay – Book 1
(four-part serial)
Part One – A Reunion
Part Two – Sparks Fly
Part Three – Christmas
Part Four – Starry Skies
Chasing Moonbeams in Merriment Bay – Book 2
Wedding Bells in Merriment Bay – Book 3

Seahorse Harbour series
Summer at my Sister's – book 1
Christmas at Aunt Elsie's – book 2
Just for Christmas – book 3
Tasty Treats at Seahorse Bites Café – book 4
Dreams and Schemes at The Seahorse Inn – book 5
Weddings and Reunions in Seahorse Harbour – book 6

Clementine Cove series
Christmas at Clementine Cove – book 1

To see a complete list of my books, or to sign up for my newsletter, go to
www.emilyharvale.com/books

If you really love my books and want to be the first to see some sneak peeks, play book related games and connect with Emily and other fans, you can ask to become a Harvale Heart and gain a virtual key to Emily's Open House.
www.emilyharvale.com/MembersClub

There's also an exclusive Facebook group for fans of my books.
www.emilyharvale.com/FacebookGroup

Or scan the QR code below to see all my books on Amazon.